also by *Meesha Mink* and *De'nesha Diamond*

Desperate Hoodwives

Shameless
Hoodwives

A Bentley Manor Tale

Meesha Mink and De'nesha Diamond

A TOUCHSTONE BOOK
PUBLISHED BY SIMON & SCHUSTER
NEW YORK   LONDON   TORONTO   SYDNEY

Touchstone

A Division of Simon & Schuster, Inc.
1230 Avenue of the Americas
New York, NY 10020

First Touchstone trade paperback edition August 2008

TOUCHSTONE and colophon are registered trademarks of Simon & Schuster, Inc.

For information about special discounts for bulk purchases, please contact Simon & Schuster Special Sales at 1-800-456-6798 or business@simonandschuster.com

Manufactured in the United States of America

10   9   8   7   6   5

Library of Congress Cataloging-in-Publication Data
Mink, Meesha.
    Shameless hoodwives : a Bentley Manor tale / by Meesha Mink and De'nesha Diamond.
        p. cm.
    "A Touchstone Book."
    1. African American women—Fiction. 2. Inner cities—Fiction. 3. Atlanta (Ga.)—Fiction. I. Diamond, De'nesha. II. Title.

PS3613.I63S53 2008
813'.6—dc22   2007036075
ISBN-13: 978-1-4165-3754-0
ISBN-10:   1-4165-3754-6

This one is for me.

—Meesha

To my baby Jordan—Momma misses you.

—De'nesha

Miz Cleo

*B*entley Manor. My hell. My prison. My home.

It's been a few months since that terrible trouble with Devani, Aisha, Lexi, Molly and, 'course, Junior. Some people still buzz about the whole mess. Me, I just shake my head and keep on keepin' on. The thing is: Trouble and Bentley Manor always go hand in hand.

This place started off as a regular Atlanta apartment complex, but in the late '70s it was the ghetto, in the late '80s the projects. Now it's the hood.

My best friend, Osceola Washington, and I laugh about that sort of stuff. We joke about how we were Bentley Manor's first Desperate Hoodwives. Together, we try to keep an eye out on things 'round here—but it don't do no good.

Folks gonna do what they wanna do.

For nearly forty years I've whittled the time away workin', strugglin', and watchin' my dreams pass me by; but with the Lord's help, I manage to hold my head high. Life is short, as they say.

Well, it is and it isn't.

Seventy-one years I've been blessed to be on this earth. I've buried parents, siblings, children, and even a husband. The young folk think hustlin' is new.

It ain't.

I've put in my hustlin' time, worked three jobs to support and raise four children. I don't know whether I've done a good job, though. I lost my oldest daughter to drugs, my two boys to the prison system, and I have no idea where the other one is.

Over the years, I've seen just about everything under the sun, which makes me wonder why I didn't see this coming. No point in being angry about it.

What's done is done.

As I lie here on this floor, watchin' the blood pour out of me, I feel a certain peace about all that's gone on before. One thang for sure: When you're dyin', your life does flash before your eyes. Now, I can't help but wonder if I coulda prevented what just happened.

Maybe I could've and maybe I couldn't. . . .

1

Takiah

I can't believe I'm moving back to Bentley Manor, but where the hell else am I going to go? All my life, I ain't had a pot to piss in or a window to throw the shit out of.

Jesus, listen to me. I got to do something about my goddamn language before I show up at my grandmother's door and she slaps the taste out my mouth.

I shift in my seat because I can't feel my ass anymore. I don't know what the fuck I was thinking, jumping on a Greyhound bus in September for seventeen hours—and with a six-month-old baby at that. I should've just fucked Dwayne so he would have fixed Kameron's Buick. Then I could've just driven me and Tanana down from Washington myself in one third the time.

Now I've just about had it with shitty looks and shitty diapers. All these motherfuckers on this bus can kiss my ass as far as I'm concerned. I paid my money just like everybody else.

Tanana squirms in my arms and I swear to God, I hold my breath, praying she doesn't wake up wailing again. I just need some peace and quiet a little while longer. My nerves are shot and I need a hit so bad I can taste it.

After a sec, she settles down and I sigh in relief. I don't have any more bottles to feed her, and she's wearing the last Pamper. Now, I'm just hoping my grandmother doesn't turn us away when we get there. Hell, I hope she's still alive.

Fuck. Why didn't I think to check before I got on this bus?

Shit. I bang my head back against the headrest and I feel tears gathering. Why don't I ever think things through? There's a sudden rumble in my stomach, followed by a long growl. Damn, when was the last time I ate anything? Two days ago?

Tears brim my eyes and I clench my teeth so hard I won't be surprised if the bastards shatter. If this plan falls through, it'll be just another fuckup in a long line of fuckups.

The major one was hookin' up with Kameron Ray,

my sorry excuse for a husband. Yeah, the nigga knows how to lay down the pipe, but he knows how to beat the shit out of me, too. Don't get me wrong, I get my licks in from time to time, but there's only so much a five-foot-four, ninety-eight-pound woman can do.

Kameron wasn't always that way. When I met him, bobbing his head at a club, I thought he was the finest piece of dark chocolate I'd ever seen. He peeped me out, too; but I was the one who bought his fine ass a drink, put on the moves by rubbing up against him, and then pretended I didn't know the power of my thick booty. Thinkin' back, I still get satin on the panties.

I'd been new to the D.C. area and I remember being surprised to see as many niggas crawlin' around that place as the A-T-L. That should have been my first clue that I had run from one hellhole to another. But, no. My ass is hardheaded. Always have been.

After grindin' up on Kameron at the club, I was satisfied I wasn't dealin' with no needle dick, and agreed to roll back to his place for some weed and more drinks. One puff told me he didn't fuck with no ordinary street shit. I'm talkin' 'bout some potent Jamaican ganja that got you so high, you thought your ass worked for NASA. For real.

I had to turn that nigga out after hookin' a sistah

up like that, but Kameron turned out to be a real freak and he was the one who turned me out. The very next day, I moved my shit into his place. A week later, Kameron pulled out some X; week after that, an eight ball.

Don't get me wrong, I hesitated at first. I've always stayed away from the heavy shit. Growin' up with my grandma in Bentley Manor, there was enough crack-heads crawlin' around that place to turn me off the shit. But Kameron started punkin' me, tellin' me he couldn't be with a bitch who didn't get down. Another clue to walk my ass out the front door. Shit, I ain't never had a nigga who could fuck me the way Kameron did, and he had enough bitches crawlin' around ready to take my spot, so what choice did I have? Hell, he coulda asked me to rob a bank and I woulda done it.

In reality, Kameron played me from the jump. Within a month, my ass was hooked on fuckin' and gettin' high. Food didn't mean shit; I rarely left his crib and I would go days without washin' my ass. Kameron's freaky ways got downright degradin' and humiliatin': whippin' and pissin' and whatnot.

I took that shit. Why? 'Cause I loved his ass; loved him like I've never loved anything in my life. That nigga took care of me. I coulda had anything I wanted, anytime I wanted it; but the only thing I wanted was Kameron.

Then came the final setup. Kameron's best friends and twins: Darrien and Dwayne came over to chill. . . .

"I'm tellin' you, dawgs. My baby can suck a dick like nobody's business," Kameron boasted, leaning his six-two body back on his Italian leather chair and puffin' on a fat blunt.

My face heated up, flattered and embarrassed he's tellin' niggas I don't even know about our business.

"No shit?" Dwayne asked, casting his high-glazed eyes over at me. *"I betcha she ain't better than that one bitch I dated last year. What was her name—Stacy, Tracy—some shit like that? Now, that bitch could suck the black off a nigga's dick."*

"Better," Kameron praised.

"I don't believe you," Darrien jumped in, eyeing me up and down like I was a car he was considering buying.

"Whatcha niggas wanna bet?" Kameron went on.

"Shit." Dwayne quickly dug into his pockets. *"I got 'bout fifty."*

I reached for Kameron's hand, my eyes asking, "What the fuck you think you doin'?"

Darrien followed his brother's lead. "I got 'bout the same."

Kameron turned innocent eyes toward me and flashed me his deep-pitted dimples. "What, baby? This is easy money."

"Can I talk to you alone for a minute?"

Irritation flashed in his eyes, but after a sec, he stood up and told the twins, "Y'all keep that money on the table, we'll be right back."

"We ain't goin' nowhere," Dwayne promised.

I quickly led the way back to our bedroom and when he closed the door, I let him have it. "What the hell is all that about?"

"What?"

"C'mon, don't play dumb. Why the hell are you telling them niggas about our business?"

Kameron's face hardened. "First of all: watch your tone. You talkin' to a grown-ass man and no bitch disrespects me—especially in my own crib."

He glared so hard at me that an apology was out of my mouth before I could think better of it.

"Just don't let the shit happen again." In a flash he's all smiles and dimples. *"Besides, what's the big deal? You give my boys a couple of blow jobs and we make some easy money."*

"Because I ain't no chickenhead. I'm supposed to be your girl."

Kameron pulled my stiff body into his arms. *" 'Course you're my girl."* He pinched my ass cheeks. *"You know how I feel about you. I love you."*

It was the first time he actually said the words and I, like a fool, instantly melted in his embrace.

"Don't I treat you good?" he asked, kissing my forehead and then the tip of my nose. *"Hmm?"*

I nodded and then accepted his lips for a soul-stirring kiss. When I came up for air, I was literally dizzy.

"If you love me, then do this shit. Make this money."

I blinked out of my stupor, still confused, but then he said the magic words.

"It'll turn me on, watchin' you do your thang. Make them niggas jealous of what I got."

This wasn't about money. This was about fulfillin' a fantasy. I smiled back. "You sure this ain't gonna change the way you feel about me?"

Laughing, he said, "Nah, baby. If anything, it's gonna make me love you more."

That sealed the deal. When we walked back out into the living room, Kameron clapped and rubbed his hands together. "You niggas got my money ready?"

I'm more than surprised that while we were in the back talking, these niggas had stripped out of their clothes and were stroking their cocks in anticipation.

"Yeah, dawg. Let's get this shit on and poppin'," *Darrien said, takin' my hand and pullin' me to the couch.*

I glanced nervously at Kameron, but he was too busy countin' to make sure all the money was there.

Both brothers pulled me down to my knees and before I knew it, I had identical cocks staring me in the eyes.

"Go ahead, baby," *Kameron encouraged.* "I'm watching you."

Okay, this is a one-time fantasy, I told my-

self, wrapping my thick lips around the closest dick in front of me. I nearly gagged on the sour smell and bitter taste. I even tried to complain; but the horny twins clamped the back of my head down, and I barely had room to breathe, let alone speak.

Behind me, Kameron started coaching like this was an Olympic sport. I started sucking and slurping like my life depended on it, ping-ponging from one cock to another.

Turned out, a blow job wasn't all the brothers wanted. Next thing I knew, my clothes were being peeled off and dicks were being shoved in every available hole I had— Kameron's dick included.

It was my first train and none of those niggas paid any attention to my tears. . . .

Sighing, new tears streak down my face, and I rush to wipe them away before this fat fucker next to me says shit. He's already spillin' all into my seat, leavin' me and Tanana with less room.

Out the window, the bus roars past a sign welcomin' us to Georgia. I relax a little bit, feelin' freedom within my grasp, though I have no idea what I'll do if Kameron gets out of jail and decides to track me down.

If. I laugh at my stupid ass for using the word. It was more like *when.*

I lost count of how many times he told me he would kill me if I ever left, never mind he has plenty of girls hustlin' the streets and jockeyin' to take my place.

I just want the fuck out. Ain't it bad enough that I don't even know who the father of my baby is?

After I backhand a few more tears, Tanana wakes wailin' for a new bottle, but I don't have one to give her.

After twenty minutes of this a few riders shout, "Shut that damn kid up!"

"Fuck you, motherfuckers!" I ain't in the mood.

An hour later, the bus finally pulls in to the Atlanta bus station, and I struggle to get off with an army of bags and a screaming baby. Lord, what I wouldn't do for a hit about now.

I nearly break my back gettin' to the nearest MARTA bus station; all the while I'm pretendin' not to notice the funk coming from Tanana's diaper. A train ride and few bus transfers later on MARTA and I'm deposited outside the iron gates of Bentley Manor.

Motherfuckin' place ain't changed a bit.

The realization causes a wave of depression to

crash through me. I walk through the gates and weave through a platoon of shaking crackheads like I'm a death row prisoner heading toward execution. When I finally stop in front of my grandma's door, my heart starts hammerin' and all I can do is stare at the door.

Before I muster the courage to knock, the knob rattles and the door swings open. After three long suffering years, I come face-to-face with my grandma Cleo. At her stunned expression I give a halfhearted cheer of, "Surprise!"

She looks faint.

2

Princess

I **don't talk much.** I guess I don't really have much to say, or better yet, I don't believe there are too many people who give a shit about what I have to say. Or think. Or believe. Or feel.

So I get shit off my chest through my pen.

Songs. Poems. Journal entries. Doodles. Notes.

Living up in Bentley Manor there is always plenty to see and write about. There's mad drama all day, every day. Like all that mess that went down a few months ago with Junior and Molly . . . and Devani . . . and Lexi . . . and Aisha. Damn, the body count was high as Iraq or some shit.

But that's Bentley Manor. You never know what's gonna be on and poppin' up in this raggedy motherfucker.

My stomach grumbles. I roll off the bed and leave my bedroom to walk into the kitchen. Last week my momma dipped for a few days and left me with not one red cent in my pocket to catch the bus to school or any food in the fridge. The only time she kept food up in here on the regular is when one of her men was around. No man—no food. I don't know what the hell the roaches and mice survivin' off of. For real.

And when she did buy food there wasn't shit but frozen dinners or pizza, Little Debbie snacks out the ass, and lots of cereal. I can't remember the last time my momma actually turned on the stove.

My foot crunches a roach as I step into the kitchen. I laugh 'cause there're dirty dishes in the sink. Now how the hell can that be without no food to cook is shot out to me. As I open the fridge I am hoping, wishing, and praying she went grocery shopping today. My lunch at school is long gone, and I'm not in the mood for another hungry night.

My disappointment tastes bitter. Ain't that a bitch?

Wasn't nothin' poppin' . . . just like this morning . . . just like last night . . . just like most of the time around here. Trust me. I thanked God for free lunch during the summer and school lunch during the rest of the year.

I slam the fridge. There ain't shit I can do with a jar filled with old grease and an empty-ass egg carton.

My momma is dead wrong for this shit. *Humph.* My momma dead wrong for a lot of shit.

I walk back to my room. I'm trying not to think of Big Macs and fried chicken as I sit on the windowsill in our second floor apartment. I sit here a lot and I see mad shit going down. Shit people care that you see and wish that you don't see. Every day up in this piece is like watching my own ghetto soap opera. Lifestyles of the poor and shameless.

Not that I don't have stories of my own. I have plenty. Memories. Nightmares. Flashbacks. A bunch of shit I wish I could forget. Shit I wish like hell never happened to me.

More strange hands than I can count have been over my body before I even had a real body. Either them triflin' motherfuckers were feeling me up, fucking me, or fucking me up.

I'm just seventeen and I know I done seen and been through way more shit than any seventeen-year-old should. Way, way more.

I feel tears rising but I swallow them bitches back, 'cause I learned early that tears didn't do shit for you. They didn't stop a grown man from taking your virginity when you were eight years old. They didn't stop your own father from beating the shit out of you like you were a stranger in the street. They didn't make your mother believe you when you tell her that another one of her string of sorry-ass boyfriends been pinching on your titties and ass.

Fuck tears.

I pick up my journal and open it. The first thing I see is a doodle of my name. Not my real name, Jamillah Unger, but my nickname, Princess. I use my finger with the bit-off nails to trace the flower pattern surrounding it. They call me Princess because my mother's nickname is Queen.

Humph. That chick ain't know shit about bein' no queen and she damn sure ain't never treat me like no princess. When my mother looks at me, she ain't seen shit but a child support check. My daddy used to beat both our asses. He's a major asshole, but he's a major asshole with a decent trucking job that pays his court-ordered support like clockwork. To me that's the only reason I'm still up in this piece. No Princess, no check.

My eyes dart out the window as raised voices float up to me.

"Bitch, where my money?"

"I ain't got it, Hassan."

See? Drama. Shit, I just got home from school. It's still early.

Hassan, one of the minor dealers up in Bentley Manor, reaches out and grabs this head name Delia by the neck. I make a face as her thin and crack-ravaged body drops to her knees as she fights to get his hands off of her.

Delia is a mess. She used to be one of the prettiest chicks I ever seen in my life. Even prettier than that chick Aisha who got slashed by one of her tricks a few months back. Delia's mixed. She's Blasian (half Black, half Asian). That crack has her ass good and jacked up. No teeth. Stank breath. Stank ass. Ashy skin. Dull eyes. Skin and bones. Walking dead.

I shift my eyes to Hassan's face. That Negro has a nasty-ass temper. Shit, I can't count how many of these heads Hassan done fucked up behind dope money. I thought this crazy-ass junkie named Smokey's ass was gonna be good and lumped the fuck up if Miz Cleo and Miz Osceola didn't run Hassan's ass off.

And I love those old ladies, especially Miz Osceola. They fightin' a losin' battle tryin' to get the drugs and the dealers up outta Bentley Manor, but you gotta give 'em an A for effort. Mind you, I just hope they don't bring the wrong attention on themselves trying to play neighborhood watch. The po-po ain't gone be worth a damn bit of help to them if one of them dealers decides to send them on to their Maker. Not that they missed much. Them two old ladies are nosy as hell, and they always tryin' to figure out the latest drama about to pop off.

A flash of red catches my eye. I look toward the building across the parking lot from me. My best friend, Lucky, is waving like crazy from her bedroom window. Is that heifer wearing a red teddy with the titties cut out? *What the fuck?*

Lucky is wild and crazy and I love her to death.

A few seconds later I see her pulling her boyfriend, Dean, in front of the window. My mouth opens as she strips him naked and then drops to her knees to take Dean's hard and long dick into her mouth.

That bitch told me in school today she was going to sneak Dean into her room to spend the night, and I didn't believe her. Leave it to Lucky to make sure she let me know I was wrong.

Her and Dean started messing around at the start of school year a few weeks ago. They been hot in each other's pants ever since. They supposed to be in love. Who knows if they really are? Shit, momma Dumb-Ass done been in love a million times since my daddy left. So much for believing in *that* shit.

Even though her mother died years ago, Lucky has

the normal teenage life I can only dream about. Boyfriends. A good relationship with her father. Thoughts of nothing but clothes, videos, and makeup. Thoughts of college when we graduate this year.

I've never had a boyfriend and don't want one. With all the men I've had playing over me when they got ready, I wasn't looking for another dude who will want to fuck me, too. All boys and men want is sex. I don't even like to bring attention to myself, so I never wear makeup and I never wear all the cute tight-fitting clothes like Lucky and most of the other girls at school. I never even think about college. I ain't smart enough and I damn sure ain't got the money. Plus I'm sure Queen will eventually throw me out once I get aged out of child support. Instead of working on a B.S. or B.A. degree, I'll be looking for a J.O.B. after I graduate.

My thin, fake-wooden bedroom door swings open suddenly.

"Princess, where Cash say he was going?"

I turn my head to see my tall and curvy redbone mother standing there. Figures the first question out her mouth would be about her latest no-good boyfriend, Cash. Fuck asking your only child about her day. Fuck making sure I went to school today.

Fuck checking to see if I ate. Fuck me. I get the picture loud and clear.

I look at her for a long time and wonder why she hates me. Is it because I look like Ben (my daddy who don't deserve to be called Daddy) or because she never wanted a kid? What is it that makes this woman treat me worse than a stepchild?

"Why you starin' at me like that?" she asks in that big booming voice of hers. "Where did Cash go?"

I just shrug my shoulders and turn my head to look back out the window. All I know is his no-good ass wasn't here when I got home and I was glad for that.

I'm 'bout tired of his ass watching me like a hawk. I flip back in my journal to the day he moved in with his garbage bag of dirty clothes. I wrote:

I hate the way he looks at me. His eyes feel like hands on me. I hate it. Another damn pervert.

He supposed to work at UPS, but the only thing I see his ass deliver is below the waist—and that's when he ain't smoking weed. He looks only a little older than me, and I don't know where she found his ugly, big teeth ass. Yesterday morning when I woke up I walked in on him and my momma having sex on the living room floor. He looked up and saw me walk in the room, and his ass ain't even stop fucking her. He just gone look up at me and wink while Momma's dumb ass steady hollering for Jesus. I just turned around and went back in my room to try and get the memory out of my head.

"Why you can't open your mouth and answer me?" Queen yells.

If I did talk would you even hear me? I think as I turn my head and look at her again.

"And why your ass always looking sad and shit?"

Bitch, like you don't know.

Queen just sucks her teeth and leaves the room, slamming the door behind her.

I flip back through the pages to the day my grandmother died. January 15, 2005. The tears come flooding back, and this time I let them fill my eyes and soak my lashes before I raise my hands to dash them away.

Granny had been my savior over the years. The few summer weeks spent at her house in South Carolina was the only time I felt any happiness. The *only* fucking time.

I bite my bottom lip as I read the letter I wrote her in my journal that day:

Dear Granny,
Today you left me and I wish that I could go
to heaven with you. I never told you that the
days I spent at your house was my lifesaver. I
could take a bath and not worry about some
man walking in on me . . . to touch me . . . to
make me touch him. At your house I knew
when I went to bed I could sleep in peace. My
door wouldn't open. The covers wouldn't be
pulled back. I wouldn't wake up with some
man hands and thing on me . . . in me.
At your house and in your arms I knew what
it meant to be loved and to be safe. Who
gonna love me now?

When she first died, I used to dream of using my hands to dig through the dirt so that I could crawl in the grave with her. The dreams stopped, but I still miss her like crazy.

I close my journal and pick up my old, taped-up, no-name CD player. I push play. The sweet strains of Mary J. Blige's classic "My Life" fill my ears and seem to drift through to my soul. I love this song.

Some of the anger I have for my momma eases . . . for now.

Some of the pain I have about my past stops . . . for now.

And some of that ache I have for my granny pauses . . . for now.

"My Life" is *my* theme song. My own cry for help. "If you look in my life and seen what I've seen," I sing, wishing and hoping and praying people really did know what the fuck I been through.

The one thing good and pure and rich in my life is my voice. Sometimes I don't feel pretty. Sometimes I know I ain't the best dressed or the smartest. But one thing I know for damn sure is that my ass can sing. It's the one thing I got from my momma that she can't take back. And I think she hates it that I sing better than her. Everybody says so.

I am getting lost in the words and the music as I sing that motherfucking song like *I* am on the mic. Like it's *my* CD. Like I'm reaching millions of people with *my* voice the way Mary J. does.

I know that my voice drifts out my open bedroom window for the wind to carry. I don't care.

I know everyone downstairs in the parking lot or in the surrounding buildings with their windows open can hear me. I don't care.

I know the pain I feel is deep in my voice. I don't care.

"Sang, Princess," someone calls up from downstairs.

Just to show off, I do a run that I know can even make Ms. Mary J. pause.

As the song ends, I open my eyes. Lucky and Dean are both in her window listening. Other people are standing to their windows. The hood boys downstairs stop shooting dice and slinging dope to look up at me. From their usual spot in front of their buildings, with their bats at their sides, Miz Osceola and Miz Cleo are listening.

My door opens again. "Will you shut the hell up and get out the window with that bullshit," Queen snaps before she slams the door again.

I ache for my mother's love so much that I hate that bitch.

3

Keisha

"Keisha, girl. You've *got* to do something about my hair!" Hawkina snatches a pink do-rag off her head and reveals a thick mess that looks like rats have been sucking on it.

"Oh, girl." I reach up to inspect the damage, but her shit is so hard, I'm surprised it doesn't cut my hand. "What the hell did you do?"

Hawkina's eyes fill with tears. "I tried this new home relaxer—"

"Say no more." I ease the door open. "C'mon, girl. Let's see if I can work a miracle." I ought to be ashamed the place is a mess, but this place always looks a mess.

My kids: Jasmine, seven; Jordan, six; Jada, five; and Jackson, four, make it impossible to keep a clean apartment. So as usual, Hawkina and I navigate our way through a floor littered with race cars, Legos, Barbie dolls, and God knows what else to make it to the kitchen where Layla is already sitting, waiting for me to base her edges.

Layla, a lanky ink-black sistah with matching eyes, glances up and does a double take on Hawkina's fried hair. "Ooh, damn, girl."

"Good morning to you, too," Hawkina says, pulling out one of my wobbly kitchen chairs and dropping her two-hundred-plus-pound ass into it.

"Damn, girl. Don't break my shit," I warn her.

Hawkina and Layla glance at each other and share a chuckle.

"Whateva," I mumble. I may have gotten most of my shit from yard sales or out by the Dumpster wheneva someone was evicted, but it is still *my* shit. I grab the red, wide-tooth comb planted in the center of Layla's thick African bush and resume parting and basing her hair.

"Now, Keisha," Hawkina starts up in a sad whine.

I already know she's about to tell me she ain't got no money.

"You know I just spent my first of the month check on school clothes for the kids. It's a few weeks late, but late is better than never. Is it all right I hook you up on the fifteenth?"

What the fuck? Don't these bitches know I got mouths to feed and clothes to buy, too? I take another glance at her jacked-up head and draw a deep breath. Heaven knows how long it's gonna take me to work on that head.

"I know you need the money, too," she adds, sliding into her best sistah-girl voice. "And if Bennie can flip some of his shipment this weekend, then I'll rush over some money sooner. Promise."

Hell, that's where her money really went: investing in pounds of marijuana like they were stock options and hoping to flip the money by selling it further south in the smaller hick towns. A bad plan; seeing how Hawkina and Bennie are going to smoke half the investment and everybody knows ain't nothin' but a bunch of meth heads in those small towns. They'll be lucky to make back what they paid for it. One thing they absolutely couldn't do is sell the shit in Bentley Manor.

M. Dawg ran the weed circuit here and Kaseem handled the harder stuff. No one, and I mean no one, tries to bite off their action. There's an order to these things and everyone respects it. That—or they get fucked up.

In all likelihood, Hawkina and Bennie will lose money, and their kids will continue to wear the same raggedy clothes they wore last year, just like mine.

"Yeah, girl. We cool," I finally say.

"Yeah?" she asks, smiling, prominently displaying her missing front teeth.

There's another knock on the front door, and I groan thinking it's somebody else wanting me to do their hair on credit, but I know good and damn well that late money makes a monkey out of no money at all.

I rush into the living room, forgetting to watch my step and nearly break my neck on a pile of jacks and marbles. "Goddammit," I hiss. How many times I got to tell these damn kids to put up their toys?

My visitor pounds on the door again. "I'm comin'!"

The banging continues, and by the time I reach the door, I'm ready to rip whoever it is a new asshole. However, when I snatch it open, my angry words die on my tongue. "Shakespeare."

The plumpest, most kissable lips God has ever created on a man curl into a smile and I feel my heart pump. Shakespeare is everything my crackhead husband ain't: dependable, reliable, and fine as hell.

"Hey, Keesh. Where's Smokey?"

"Where you think? 'Sleep." I laugh, but my voice is absent of humor.

Shakespeare glances at his watch and shakes his head. "He had an appointment with his parole officer this morning."

Typical. "He ain't said shit to me about it." I point to the bedroom. "You're more than welcome to try and wake him up if you wanna."

Releasing a frustrated sigh, Shakespeare navigates effortlessly through the maze of toys and heads toward the back. "Afternoon, ladies."

"Hey, Shakespeare," my kitchen-saloon customers chime.

Layla and Hawkina grin and wink at Shakespeare as he passes. When he disappears into the bedroom, the women collapse against each other, giggling.

"All right. You ladies behave," I chastise, tumbling over an endless stream of toys. "Goddammit," I shout when I almost pitch face forward over Jordan's skates.

Just then, Jasmine, my oldest, rushes through the door. "I saw Uncle Shakespeare. Is he here?"

"Where's your brothers and sister at?" I snap instead. "You guys need to get in here and pick up these damn toys."

Jasmine's eager face falls and nearly rips my heart out. When will I learn to stop taking my frustrations out on the kids? "Yeah, he's here," I say, softening my voice. "But go get your brothers and sister and come clean this mess up. Uncle Shakespeare will still be here when you get back."

Jasmine's face lights up again. "Okay. I'll be right back." She disappears back out the door.

Shaking my head, an amused smile claims my lips as I turn back toward the kitchen. The girls have already returned to their seats, but are still snickering about my brother-in-law.

"Keisha, girl. Why in the hell did you ever hook up with Smokey's triflin' behind when you coulda had Shakespeare's fine ass?"

"Girl, hush," I say, snatching her head back to finish basing.

"Ow. Chile, watch it," Layla snaps. "You know I'm tender-headed."

"Sorry."

Hawkina laughs. "She ain't sorry. She's just mad she picked the wrong brother." She attempts to cross those thick ham hocks she calls legs, but after a few failed attempts, she settles on just crossing her ankles and letting her knees point in opposite directions. "Hell, I'm kicking my damn self. You know Shakespeare had a crush on me back in high school."

I can't help but laugh at that bullshit. "Come on,

now, Hawkina. Everybody knows Shakespeare has only been crazy about one girl his whole life."

Layla bobs her head, agreeing. "Devani. Her over-reaching ass. If you ask me, she got what was coming to her."

"Stop it now. It's not nice to speak ill of the dead."

"Humph," Hawkina grumbles under her breath. "She ain't saying nothing we didn't say when Devani was walking around this motherfucker. Always had her nose in the air, acting like she was too good for this place, just 'cause she had gone to some damn technical schools and was fucking a football player.

"We all know that nigga had something to do with that drive-by shooting. Geneva said that she heard from Afrika that the bitch was also pregnant."

"Hawkina!" I glance up to make sure Shakespeare isn't around to hear.

"What? I'm just speaking the truth. Zion said that she recognized Tyrik's black SUV that night of the shooting."

I perk up at this news. "Did she tell the police?"

Hawkina's face twists into an expression that clearly says, "Have you lost your damn mind? Ain't nobody tellin' the po-po shit. They spend too much time up in this motherfucker as it is."

My face flushes with embarrassment. Hawkina

didn't say it, and she didn't need to, but Smokey and I are one of the reasons the police roll up in here on the regular. It usually goes something like: Smokey would score some crack, come home and think his ass was runnin' shit, and try to beat my ass.

It usually sounds like a war in this motherfucker. Next thing I know, Miz Cleo is on the phone and Smokey is off to cool his heels in a holding cell. I never press charges, not because I enjoy the occasional black eye, but because Smokey . . . well, because I love the bastard.

At least, I used to.

Now?

This shit is gettin' old. I'm not being wishy-washy; but I fell in love with Smokey back when we were in high school, back when the hardest thing he smoked was a couple of blunts. Believe it or not. He was once cute himself. Six-two, lean, and the captain of the basketball team. Hell, I was the captain of the cheer-leading squad. Back then, it just made sense for us to be together.

Then came the bum knee.

Then the never-ending pity party.

Then shortly before graduation, I got pregnant.

Two hours after I received my diploma, I was standing in Fulton County courthouse, getting married. My momma cried through the whole ceremony. Wailing about how I was screwing up my life. At the time, I thought I was doing much better than her. She'd never been married and claimed a different man was my father damn near every year of my life.

I was doing good. I had a ring around my finger.

Joke's on me; especially after the first year Smokey turned to crack, he'd slipped my precious ring off my finger while I was asleep and sold it.

In my mind, we were like Whitney and Bobby. I was going to love him to recovery. Our vows meant the world to me. Sure, there had been a few times when I'd get mad, pack up the kids, and head out to my sister's house out in the suburbs, but I would always come back. Somebody has to look after Smokey.

At least my sister, Cheryl, made it out of Bentley Manor.

My ass will probably die here.

A commotion in the living room draws me out of my private thoughts. I look up and see Shakespeare trying to aid my husband to one of the wicker chairs in the living room. Smokey, with one arm wrapped around his brother's shoulders, looks more like a puppet than a man.

"Shit," I mumble and then stop smoothing in Layla's relaxer. "I'll be right back."

Of course the kids hadn't returned to pick up their things and, this time, I end up kickin' a Tonka truck.

Shakespeare curses under his breath as he finally deposits Smokey in a chair. "He can't go in like this. His P.O. will have a fit and make him take a drug test."

Then he'll be arrested for parole violation and then finally out of my hair. The second I complete the thought, I feel guilty. What happened to my loyalty?

My gaze caresses my husband's face. He looks so calm—so blissful. I don't understand, but a love comes over me; not the sort of love a wife has for a husband, but the kind of love a mother has for a child. I've been protecting Smokey for so long I don't know how to do anything else.

"So what are we going to do?" I ask.

Anguish twists Shakespeare's face as he runs his hands over his braids. "I don't know. I gotta come up with some bullshit story." He heads toward the door.

If anyone can come up with something, it's Shakespeare. He's a talented writer who just landed his first publishing contract. *He* is going to make it out of Bentley Manor, too.

Maybe I did fall for the wrong brother.

"I'll call you on my cell after I talk to his parole officer," he tells me at the door. "Wish me luck."

"Good luck." Instead of immediately closing the door, I watch him as he rushes down the dingy hallway. Bless his heart. Shakespeare is truly his brother's keeper. It's hard to imagine what this place will be like without him.

"Keisha! How long are you gonna leave this shit in my head?"

I roll my eyes and finally close the door. When I turn around and face the wicker chair, I'm convinced my eyes are playing tricks on me.

But they're not.

While Smokey is fast asleep, a long stream of piss seeps from beneath the oval wicker chair and forms a big puddle on the carpet.

"I'm so over this shit."

4

Woo Woo

How can I explain the way Hassan makes me feel? How the fuck do I put into words how his touch ain't like shit I've ever felt before? Nothing or no one can fuck with it. Why else am I out and about at this time of the night?

My heart is pounding and my thong's already wet with my juices before I even knock on his door. As soon as it opens, I get lost in those hazel green eyes as his hand reaches out to lightly grab my neck and pull me inside the dark apartment. I pant like a dog as he presses my body back against the wall by the closed door. He snatches open the black Claiborne trench coat I'm wearing. I came ready to be fucked like no one else can fuck me. The streetlamps show through the first-floor windows, revealing the black lace teddy I'm wearing.

With one strong tug, he tears that flimsy-ass lace from my body and flings it across the room. That shit cost me seventy bucks from Frederick's and trust me, I don't give a fuck that it's ruined. As he presses his soft lips to my neck I bring my hands up to stroke his braids. I tingle all over as his tongue traces a path down to circle my rock-hard nipples.

"Yes. Oh God, yes," I whisper as I push my ass against the wall and then squat my legs.

He knows what I want.

His hands shift up my quivering thighs to palm my whole pussy before he massages it like a tight muscle. "Damn, you wet," he moans against my tit before he sucks it deeper into his warm and wet mouth.

I place my hands on both sides of his face and look him dead in the eyes. "Make it wetter," I whisper against his lips before I suck his whole mouth into mine.

His hands come up to deeply rub both of my breasts as he kisses me softly before he deepens the kiss with his tongue. I love to kiss Hassan. That shit is perfect. Not too wet. Not too hard. It's all slow and freaky. Hassan knows just what a woman wants.

His fingertips roll and twist my nipples as he massages my breasts. My pussy lips go to smacking. He presses one of his jean-covered legs between my legs and grinds my pussy against it. I love the hard pressure against my throbbing clit.

As he pushes both my titties up with his hands and suckles my nipples some more, I rotate my hips like I'm working a damn stripper pole.

"Go on and make that pussy cum so I can lick it up," he whispers in that raspy voice of his that I love.

My ass slaps against the wall as I grind and slide across his leg like I'm truly riding a dick. His hands come down to tightly grasp my butt as he pushes that leg up against my pussy again.

The dam finally breaks and explodes inside of me as sweat covers my body and my heart feels like it's coming out of my damn chest. "I'm cuuuuuummmmmmmmmming," I yell out all hoarse and shit while I shake like a junkie needing a fix. Fuck it. My ass damn sure is addicted to Hassan.

He drops to his knees and puts my legs on his shoulders before he brings his hands up to my thighs to press my legs up. I'm flexible as hell, and that move brings all that good pussy right in his face as my knees touch the wall next to my shoulders. "Smells good," he moans before he licks from my asshole to the top of that pussy like it's ice cream on a hot summer day.

I tease my own nipples as Hassan eats me like a true professional. He sucks the plump lips and then licks them. He puts sweet hickies on the top of that bald motherfucker. He kisses my clit and then licks it with that tongue trick of his that drives me crazy. He pushes three fingers inside me one by one and then sucks the wetness from them like he's starving. He circles my asshole with the tip of his tongue and then blows cool air up my ass until I buck against his face.

See . . . how do I explain how good this shit is?

This nigga got me good and fucked up.

He releases my legs. I drop them to the floor. When I try to stand on them, I wobble and shit. "If you want the dick you better come and get it," he tells me over his shoulder as he walks into his bedroom.

Oh, I want it. I want it bad.

I kick off my Gucci "fuck me" heels. I'm scared I'm gone fall, so I hold myself up against the wall as I try like hell to make it to his room in the darkness on shaky-ass legs. If I have to walk through hell with a can of gas strapped to my ass to get to that room, then I will.

Ever since my crackhead momma left me and my sister Lexi with our nana, I've been calling Bentley Manor home. My spot. My hood. I learned some of the best and worst shit I know right up in that crazy-ass complex.

I learned how to whup ass and talk shit there. At twelve, I sneaked and smoked my first cigarette in the stairwell of our building. At fourteen, I smoked my first blunt at my friend Sasha's apartment. At fifteen, my hot ass finally got some of that good stuff in boys' pants (thank God it got better with age). The first time I lived alone was when I took over my grandmother's apartment in Bentley Manor. When I graduated high school and then technical college, my ass was right up in the Manor.

Shit, I remember plenty of late nights when we all would hang out in the parking lot drinking and smoking weed, talking shit, and telling jokes. In the summertime we would get water guns like big-ass kids and chase each other in and out of the apartments.

But there been some bad shit, too. Some real bad shit. Murders. Violence. Drug busts. Newborn babies thrown away like trash. Robberies. Crazy shit.

I still get sick when I think of how close my sister came to killing her faggot-*ass*, on-the-down-low-*ass*, no-good-son-of-a-bitch-*ass* husband. Emphasis on ass since that's what he likes so damn much. Walking in on Lexi holding that gun on Luther almost made me shit my damn pants that day.

Yeah, I've had some good- and bad-ass times in Bentley Manor, but I always thought once I was out of that motherfucker I wouldn't come back. Hell, my nana been dead going on ten years. I ain't seen my bitch of a mother in God knows when. My sister moved her kids into their own house outside Atlanta. I moved out of my apartment the same day Reggie proposed three months ago. I left so fast that I didn't get all my deposit back. From the hood to the burbs where life is all good. And I thought that day was the last day I would see Bentley Manor.

But I do go back. It's always late at night while most people are asleep. So no one can see me. So that no one will know. I park my car down the street and walk into the complex to head straight to Hassan's apartment.

Just like last night.

I shiver as I think of the things he did—*we* did to each other. It was worth it. Fuck it. Even though I overslept because I didn't want to leave his bed or his arms, it was worth it. I was almost late for one of the most important days in my life . . . but it was *still* worth it.

And it was significant because it was the last time I would ever allow myself to see that nigga again. So hell, yeah, last night was worth everything I risked.

"Aleesha . . . Aleesha?"

I shake myself from my thoughts. "Yes?"

I hear a slight rumble of laughter behind me.

"I *said* do you, Aleesha Moore, take this man, Reginald Carver, to be your lawfully wedded husband?" Reverend Yarborough asks.

I feel nervous as hell. Through my sheer wedding veil, I look up at my boyfriend of the last three years and lick my glossy lips. He smiles down at me and squeezes my hand. He's a good man. A hardworking man who wants nothing more than to give me a good life. A good marriage.

"I do," I say, as I look up into his warm brown eyes.

We are as different as night and day.

He's suburbs. I'm hood.

He's laid back. I'm wild and crazy.

He walks the straight and narrow. I like my Crown Royal straight and my blunts rolled wide.

He's never given me a reason to think he's cheated on me, and I can't count a solid length of time where I didn't have a dick on the side—a backup plan; a security blanket; an escape route.

I know that he loves me and I *do* love him.

"By the power vested in me by our Lord and Savior and by the state of Georgia I now gloriously and joyously pronounce you Aleesha Moore and you Reginald Carver as husband and wife for now and forevermore."

Reggie raises my veil over my head and lowers his head to kiss me. I close my eyes and try like hell not to compare his warm and fuzzy sexuality to that heated fire I have with Hassan.

Uh . . . *had* with Hassan. Had.

5

Keisha

By nature, I'm not a morning person. When I wake up, I feel like my arms and legs are being held down by weights; my tongue glued to the roof of my mouth, and I even manage to rip a few eyelashes out by their roots, tryna pry my eyes open. This morning, I'm a little disoriented because I can't understand, for the life of me, what the hell I'm looking up at.

After blinking a few times, I realize it's a bed, but that doesn't make sense. Something moves beside me and then a small hand plops against my face. Now I remember. I'm in one of the children's bunk beds. Jordan had a nightmare last night and wouldn't go back to bed unless I went with him.

I try to sit up. When I do, I realize my nightgown

is wet and plastered against my skin. Apparently Jordan had a little accident.

Like father, like son.

I groan under my breath and pry myself out of bed. Since there's only one bathroom in this shitty apartment, I'll shower and change first, then come back and get him cleaned up.

It's early, and though most children are probably up and watching Saturday morning cartoons, my kids sleep in, certainly not because they don't like cartoons, but because we don't have a TV.

We can't.

Smokey keeps pawning the motherfucker. It's also the reason why we don't own stereos, iPods, disc players, any kind of kitchen appliances—except for the refrigerator and stove, and that's because those are too heavy for Smokey to carry out of here.

We're down to the bare bones—the essentials. Sure, from time to time other things come up missing: furniture, toys, and sometimes socks. Hell, I went through one period when Smokey sold my underwear. Now who the fuck wants to buy someone else's raggedy drawers?

It's a damn shame, I know, but after a while, you get used to it.

I make the short journey to the bathroom, not

bothering to check to see whether Smokey made it in last night. In truth, I'm not ready to deal with him right now, especially after he embarrassed me.

And in front of Hawkina.

Now everybody is going to know our business. Not that they don't know already.

I flip on the bathroom switch and grumble at the sight of Smokey's clothes lying all over the damn place. I swear nobody in this bitch picks up after themselves. Before I jump on a soap box, let me calm the fuck down. Bitchin' ain't gonna solve nothin'.

After peelin' my pissy gown off, I stop and stare at the mirror. I barely recognize the woman looking back at me. What happened to my slim, curvy, cheerleader's body I had just eight years ago? My once perky breasts now look like a couple of flat tires; my waist has expanded and left me with a small pouch beneath my belly button. My thighs are a little thicker and I try like hell not to notice how my arms jiggle. Overall, I'm not fat, but I ain't slim either.

My face is another story. At twenty-six I look a good ten years older, maybe a little more than that. What the fuck will I look like in five more years? Ten?

Tears spring outta nowhere, and the woman in the mirror's face twists and contorts into something that ain't pretty.

Trust me.

Crying turns into sobbing, and then the next thing I know I can't stop. I slump down onto the bathroom floor, hugging my knees and rocking back and forth. God, what I wouldn't give to turn back the hands of time. To have it all to do over again.

"Momma?"

Jackson's voice floats out to me, and I quickly scramble around the floor and shut the door. I don't want my baby catchin' me like this. A few seconds later, he knocks.

"Momma?"

"Y-yes, baby?" To stop him from comin' in, I press my naked body against the door just as he turns the knob. "Momma's not dressed right now, honey."

There's a long silence, but I know he hasn't moved away from the door. Instead, he tries the knob again.

I finally press the small lock button and move away. "Jackson, go and play with your toys. Momma's fixna take a shower. I'll make ya somethin' to eat in a minute."

After another long silence, Jackson shuffles away. I'm sad to say it's not the first time we've done this. Sometimes he'll ask if Daddy hit me again or whether I hit his daddy. What the hell am I supposed to say to that shit?

My other three stopped askin' me about my cryin' fits and now acted like such things are no more unusual than me washin' dishes or doin' laundry. Fuckin' great example, huh?

After a few minutes, my tears dry and I manage to get off the floor. This time, I avoid the mirror and head toward the shower. I need to make it quick and get breakfast started.

I yank back the green shower curtain and scream at the sight of a naked body slumped in the tub. I don't even check who it is before I race out the bathroom door. Hell, I don't give a shit. When I smack into something hard, I think my dumb ass has just hit a wall. But then it speaks.

"Keesh, what is it?"

I whip my head around and I'm stunned shitless to see Shakespeare. "What the fuck?" My eyes roam over him like I'm expecting him to change into someone else.

"What is it?" he asks again; his concerned gaze rakes over me and I remember: I'm butt-naked.

"Shit." I race to my bedroom. When I slam the door behind me, I quickly lock and slump against it. Pantin', I can't believe what just happened. Shakespeare just saw me naked. I glance across my cluttered bedroom to the dresser's mirror and shudder with disgust.

From the other side of the door, I hear the children cryin',' and I remember the body in the tub and my crazy screamin'. I quickly grab some clothes from off the floor. No, they're not clean, but nothing is since I haven't had time to do laundry. In record time, I'm back out the door and pushin' my way through the kids to reach the bathroom.

"Y'all go and play," I snap.

Of course, nobody moves.

Shakespeare is hunched over the tub and smacking Smokey's face, tryna wake him up. Shit. With a racing heart, I manage to squeeze closer. There's something about Smokey's ashen complexion that scares me. Is this it? Has he killed himself?

Am I finally free?

My knees bang against the bathroom's cheap linoleum as I also lean over and jab my finger up against Smokey's neck for a pulse.

"C'mon, bro. Wake up." A few more smacks, and then Shakespeare asks, "He scored last night?"

"Shit. I don't know." I can't help but be irritated by the question. I'm doin' the best I can. Hell, I can't babysit Smokey's ass twenty-four/seven. Why does he keep expectin' me to?

I feel a pulse. It's faint, but it's there. My body

slumps, though I'm not sure if it's relief or disappointment I feel.

"Is Daddy dead?" Jasmine's trembling voice reaches my ear and I turn around to see the kids are still gathered at the door, watching us like hawks.

"No, Daddy is fine," I say, climbin' back to my feet. Behind me, Shakespeare keeps smackin' and pleadin' for his older brother to wake up. "He's just restin' right now." I usher them out of the cramped bathroom and literally have to push them into the living room.

It's a shame they have to see their father like this; however, it's no different than them watching their dad tremble, shake, and beg people in the street for money. Other kids tease them, but it ain't like Smokey is the only crackhead in Bentley Manor.

Far from it.

That doesn't mean I don't stop worrying about how all this shit affects my kids. Hell, I worry about it every damn day. But again, what the fuck am I supposed to do? Leave Smokey? Let him kill himself?

Yeah, I know. He'll probably do that shit anyway. The real truth is: we don't have anywhere else to go.

Momma's diabetes took her out a couple of years ago, and my bougie-ass sister has made it painfully clear how she feels about me and the kids staying at her crib. Bitch acts like she's always had money.

Fuckin' sellout.

"Who wants pancakes?"

"I do, I do," my greedy kids chorus.

I shuffle toward the kitchen, painfully aware I still smell like piss, but I can only handle one thing at a time. When I enter the kitchen, I get another shock: the damn stove is gone.

Fuck.

"Thanks for buying us a new stove," I tell Shakespeare. "I'll get the money back to you . . . somehow."

"Don't worry about it. It's my job to see after you guys." He laughs.

"It's not your job."

"It's my job to look after my brother and his family."

I laugh, mainly because his is so infectious. "You're still trying to be your brother's keeper?"

"It's not such a bad job." He shrugs. "I don't mind."

"Keisha!"

I turn to see Afrika waving me down. "Gurl, can you fix my braids?"

"Yeah. Just give me a minute." I turn back to Shakespeare.

He shakes his head. "Why don't you go to hair school or something? Get a license so you can set up a real shop."

"School?" I laugh. "How in the hell am I supposed to go to school?"

A shirtless Shakespeare flashes me a smile before loading up another box into the rented U-Haul. "Damn, Keesh. I didn't say you should run for president. Going to school isn't impossible. I did it."

"You ain't got four kids and a crackhead husband either," I snap. I glance around the complex, disgusted by how it looks like one huge landfill: cans, broken crack vials, beer bottles, and just plain trash everywhere. Plus, there are more cars jacked up on c-blocks than ones that actually run in this motherfucker. This place depresses me. It's the sort of depression that gets deep into your soul and festers.

Shakespeare places another box on the truck, and I wish like hell I was the one moving out. But like I said, I'll probably die here.

Just then, Jasmine walks out of the apartment building, lugging a heavy box. "Can I put this in the truck, Uncle Shakespeare?"

We both notice the strain of her arm muscles and,

bless her heart, how her knobby knees look like they're ready to buckle.

"Here, honey. Let me help you with that." Her uncle rushes to her side.

"No. No. I got it," Jasmine protests.

Shakespeare backs off, but shadows close behind just in case she truly does need help. I smile. He's really good with kids.

Why couldn't Shakespeare have been their father?

He flashes me another smile, and my heart flip-flops like a teenager in love. Damn. What in the hell is wrong with me? Fantasizing about this type of shit will get my ass in trouble. I know it.

Jasmine finally sets the box on the truck and receives a fatherly peck against the forehead as a reward. Jealousy curls in my stomach. How ridiculous is that?

Jasmine takes off back toward the building, probably to grab another box.

Shakespeare turns his sparkling brown eyes toward me.

"Look, Keesh. You hook up just about everybody's head up in here for damn near pennies and sometimes for free. You have a talent. You need to try and capitalize on it."

There he goes talkin' like those uppity college Negroes again. I can't help but roll my eyes. "You always make shit sound so easy."

"School is never easy," he admits, his muscles flexin' as he grabs another box. "But it's always worth it."

"Uh-huh." I jab my hands against my hips. "Schools cost money. The last time I checked I ain't eatin' paper and shittin' money."

There's a sudden intensity to his dark gaze and it sort of contradicts his casual shrug. "I'll pay for it."

I'm completely thrown for a loop. "You?"

Another shrug. "Why not? I got my advance check from my book contract. I'll be happy to pay for it."

He's actually serious, I realize. Still, I can't help but laugh. "Yeah. Right."

"C'mon, Devani . . ."

My head snaps up.

"I mean, Keisha." He laughs at the slip. "Won't you at least think about it?"

I've never liked the thought of charity, despite the fact I'm in serious need of it.

"Please?" he adds.

Hell, it won't hurt to think about it, but I already know what my answer's gonna be.

He cocks his head and gives me his best puppy-dog expression.

"Fine. Fine. I'll *think* about it."

"Good."

He leans over and plants a kiss against my cheek. It was nothing but a brotherly peck, but there's a strange fluttering in the pit of my stomach all the same.

"You all right?" he asks, staring curiously at my flushed face.

"Uh, yeah," I cover lamely. "Never better." The minute he turns away to grab another box, I place a hand against my tingling cheek and sigh like a silly schoolgirl.

6

Takiah

I love her, but Grandma Cleo is already gettin' on my nerves. Sure, she acts like she's happy to see me and Tanana and all; but damn, she asks too many questions. Where have I been? How come I never called? Where did I get these bruises? Where's my husband? When was the last time I ate?

On and on.

The shit is old, and it's only been forty-eight hours. Grandma Cleo's friend, Miz Osceola—Miz Nosceola, I call her—sure don't look too damn happy to see my black ass back here. Every time she looks at me, her nose twitches like she smells something nasty—probably her bottom lip.

We never did get along.

Growing up, Miz Osceola hovered around and

poked her nose in my business like she was my damn momma or something. Shit, it's hard enough growing up knowing my own momma didn't want jack to do with me; I didn't need remindin'.

Hell, being back in this hellhole is like traveling back in time. The minute I entered the apartment, I feel like a pawned-off orphan again. . . .

"Momma is gonna go away for a little while."

At five years old I stared up into my mother's red, swollen eyes and knew this would be the last time I would ever see her.

I wrapped my small arms around her knees. "Nooo. Don't go." My gaze cut to the scary man standing in Granny's doorway. I don't know who he is, but he had the greasiest hair I had ever seen and he wore so much black leather, he squeaked when he walked. He looked bored and ready to go.

"Why can't I go with you?" I asked. "I'll be good. Promise."

"I'm sorry, sweetie. Momma gotta go and see about a job. If I get it, then I'll be able to save up enough money to get us our own place. Wouldn't you like that?"

The question doesn't make sense. How

come we can't just live with Granny? She won't mind.

"C'mon, Ruthie," the ugly man by the door said. "We ain't got all night."

"I'm comin'," Momma snapped over her shoulder, then faced me with a smile too big for her face. "Now, I want you to promise to be a big girl and mind your granny."

My vision blurred with hot tears. She was truly gonna leave me. First Daddy left to go to prison and now this. Instead of promising, I tightened my arms around her legs and sobbed.

"C'mon, baby. Now don't be like this."

Momma is getting angry, but I didn't care. I wanted to go, too.

Momma pulled at my arms, but when she was unable to get me to let go, another set of arms grabbed me from behind.

"Come on, baby. Your momma has to go."

It's Grandma Cleo, sounding about as sad as I felt. Surely she didn't believe momma was coming back.

"Ruthie," the ugly man barked.

"Why don't you just leave us alone," I screamed. "She doesn't want to go with you!"

The man just laughed. "I'll go wait out in the car." He looked up at Momma. "Just don't have me waiting out there too long."

I'm glad to see him go. So much so, that I managed to escape Granny's firm grip to race to the door and lock it.

"Oh, baby." Momma knelt down. "Lockin' the door doesn't change anything. I still have to go." She pulled me in her arms and we hugged as if our lives depended on it.

"You're coming back, right?" I asked, hoping I'm wrong about it being our last time together.

"Of course I'm coming back. Wild horses couldn't keep me away."

In the end, I was right. I never saw my mother again.

"Takiah, honey, it's past noon," Grandma Cleo says, cracking open my door.

We both know that's code for me to get my lazy ass out of bed and come take care of my baby. I groan because this bed is feeling too good and I can't remember the last time I've been able to just sleep in like this. "Can I have just a few more minutes?" I plead.

Hell, it ain't gonna kill her to watch Tanana just a little while longer.

"Honey, one of us is gonna hafta go to the store and buy this baby some food and diapers. The ones I borrowed from Angie across the way are just about gone."

Shit. "I ain't got any money, Granny."

"Chile, I know that. I didn't fall off the turnip truck yesterday. Now, get on up so I can go to the store. I don't have a car seat or I would take her with me."

"Yes, ma'am," I say, knowing any other response would get me in trouble. I ignore my body, poppin' and protestin' as I climb out of bed. I can barely walk a straight line as I head out of my old bedroom. When she hands Tanana over, I notice how she looks and smells brand new.

I guess a good, hot bath will do that.

I'm suddenly aware of my own tart b.o., and I'm thinking about begging Granny to hold up running to the store so I can splash some water on my ass, but almost immediately after handing me Tanana, she's out the door.

Alone at last.

I plop down on the sofa, ignoring the scrunch of Granny's beloved plastic. Damn, she still has this shit on here? This don't make no kind of sense. This sofa has to be older than I am, but looks brand new. I don't know why, but I laugh.

As my gaze zooms around the living room, I'm struck by how nothing has changed in this small place since I moved out. Hell, since I moved in. Seriously, it's like being trapped in some kind of time machine, but crazy shit like this is why I love Grandma Cleo.

Life keeps throwing me bricks, but Granny stays the same. The same person. The same love. The same acceptance.

I can't say the same for Bentley Manor.

Tanana squirms to get out of my lap and I let her down. Instantly, a large smile covers my child's face and the effect is like a burst of sunshine in my soul, but just as quickly a cloud dampens my spirits.

After all the shit I've done in my life, I don't deserve such a beautiful child. Yet, here she is—perhaps a little small for six months, but she's a happy child.

Tanana rarely cries, the long bus ride being an exception. I'm jealous of her thick, wavy hair, large almond-shaped eyes, and curly lashes. She's at least two shades darker than my dull clay-brown coloring and two shades lighter than Kameron's dark chocolate.

But with parents with souls as black as ours, what chance does my baby really have in this world?

Unexpected tears brim my eyes and fear seizes my heart. I don't want my baby to turn out like me. I mean, I'm a mess. Always have been. I was stealing from the local Circle K at seven, drinking at ten, smoking pot and having sex by twelve, and this was despite my grandma and her Bentley Manor spies.

How am I going to do better by my child?

While I'm stuck on this question, I watch Tanana crawl all over the place and suddenly I feel like I'm in over my head.

I certainly hadn't done any better since I escaped Grandma's watchful eyes either. Sure, I can sit here and blame Kameron, but he didn't put a gun to my head. Well, at least not at first. My decline into becoming a junkie had little to do with the desire to get high and everything to do with my looking for unconditional love.

But love made a fool out of me, Kameron convincing me to let him and his boys run a train on me was just the beginning. After that, it wasn't long before a few of his other friends wanted to try me out. Suddenly, my man was teaching me tricks, coaching me on how to guarantee his boys would keep coming back for more, turning me into a certified ho. And those girls I thought were sweatin' for my spot were just his other hos lining his pockets, supporting our drug habit.

I might have given a fuck if I wasn't high all the

damn time. I might have done a lot of things different if that had been the case. Hell, the first time I overdosed didn't even cure me. How pathetic is that? I woke up in the hospital jonesing for another hit.

Kameron was right by my side, hooking me up wheneva the nurses left the room. At the time, I thought it was a sign of true love. My man didn't want to see me hurting like that.

Shit.

Someone should have just stamped the word "fool" across my head and be done with it. The few times I did try to leave, Kameron transformed from the happy-go-lucky man I fell in love with to the nigga with a mile-long rap sheet who wouldn't think twice to stomp your ass into the ground to keep you from shortening his pockets.

Around the third time he'd broken my arm and blackened my eye, I understood: I was a piece of property and Kameron was my master.

Grandma Cleo was wrong about one thing: I had tried to call—once. One of my johns had left his cell phone in one of the hotel rooms Kameron rented out on the regular; I'd nervously hid in the cramped bathroom, dialing my grandma's number I knew by heart. The line just rang while my heart ticked so loudly, it sounded like something attached to explosives. It being the middle of a Saturday afternoon, I knew my granny was likely sitting out on her stoop and minding everybody's business but her own.

Shaking my head of those long-ago memories, I'm still stuck with my original question. How in the hell do I go about making a better life for my child when I'm so fucked up?

"Lord, help," I mumble under my breath. "Can't you just send me some kind of sign?"

A loud knock on the front door nearly causes my bones to jump out of my skin.

Kameron!

The sofa's plastic rips the light hairs from my bare legs as I bolt straight up. I ignore the pain and rush across the floor and grab Tanana. Hell, I didn't think he would be out of jail so damn fast. What am I going to do?

There's another fierce pounding on the door, and I scan my surroundings for a hiding place. My hold on my baby tightens as I consider making a run for the front window. It wouldn't be so bad. The apartment is on the first floor.

Tanana blasts a mighty wail, letting me know I'm scaring her.

"Miz Cleo?" a heavy baritone seeps through the closed front door.

Tears splash down my face in relief. It's not Kameron.

"Miz Cleo?" the man asks again, knocking. "Is everything all right in there?"

"Just a second." I prop Tanana up on my hip and march toward the front door, ignoring the fact the only clothes I have on is an old Redskins jersey that just barely reaches mid-thigh and some holey Wal-Mart underwear.

The visitor was in mid-knock when I finally snatch the door open. "Pastor Meyer."

A cool even smile spreads across Pastor Eddie Meyer's face while his eyes drink me in. "Well. Well. Look who's all grown up now." He chuckles good-naturedly. "Is your grandma here, Takiah? She called and said that she wanted an emergency prayer session."

I roll my eyes. "She probably wanted you to lay hands on me and cast out demons."

The pastor's brows rise with open curiosity. "If that's what you need to find your way, child, I'm nothing but the Lord's humble servant." His smile widens. "May I come in?"

7

Princess

hate the weekends. Although I ain't doing the best I can in high school, it gives me a break from this raggedy-ass apartment. With Cash sitting his bony ass 'round here, I try to find something to do or somewhere to go whenever my momma leaves for work.

I eventually learned not to leave myself alone with no man . . . especially any of *her* men. So if I have to sit in the hall till my momma get home to keep from being alone with *her* man, then I will sit my ass in the hall alone. Even if it means listening to her talking shit 'cause I didn't stay home like she told me. I rather hear her mouth than have *her* man looking at me like he ready to fondle and fuck me.

So all morning I stay in my room and write in my journal as Momma and Cash stay holed up in theirs.

She all caught up in *her* man, living life like I don't exist, but there ain't shit new about that. That shit old as time.

I worked on a new song today called "Me and Mines." It's about a woman with a child and how she makes the men respect her and her child.

I wish my momma would put me first in her life. "That's a fucking joke," I mutter as I doodle in the book. The one time I got the nerve to tell her the truth, I found out my momma was a no-good bitch.

"Roy, baby, I'm gone to the corner store real quick. You want something?" Queen asked.

I was in my bedroom but I dropped my doll to the cold floor to go and stand at the living room entryway. My momma was slipping on her winter wool coat as she smiled at her boyfriend Roy like he was Jesus.

I ran to my room and grabbed my dingy jean coat. I barely took time to put it on before I ran back to the living room. "Can I go, Momma?" I asked, coming to stand beside her as she stood at the front door.

"Girl, go sit down. You ain't got to move every damn time I move. Shit," Queen snapped, her eyes angry as she looked down at me.

I glanced back at Roy, sitting on our old ratty green couch already sipping on beer. "Please, Momma. Please," I begged as tears filled my eyes.

"What the hell you crying for?" she yelled.

"Queen, go on to that store. She'll be just fine with me," Roy slurred from his spot on the couch.

"Momma, please don't leave me. Please," I cried, dropping to my knees as I held on to her coat like my life depended on it.

WHAP!

I gasped as she backhanded me. I fell back to the floor. My face stung from the ring on her hand.

She slammed out the house.

Roy was on me like white to rice. He picked me up from the floor and tried to stroke my hair while his hands went down inside my panties. I turned my head and bit the shit out of his salty-tasting hand as he blew his beer breath in my face. He dropped me and I hollered out as my six-year-old body hit the floor with a thud.

The front door swung open and my mother stood there. "What's going on?"

Roy held his hand out to her. "She bit me when I tried to make her get off the floor, hollering and carrying on," he lied.

My momma's eyes dropped on me like a load of bricks.

"He lying, Momma," I yelled, looking at him with eyes full of hate. "He touched my stuff. He always touch my stuff when you gone."

"Princess, you gone lie on me 'cause I told you to stop crying?" he asked, sounding offended as he looked down at me. He turned to my momma standing there with her hand on her hip. "Queen, I take care of this girl like she mine and she gone lie on me like that. Man, let me get the fuck outta here 'fore y'all get a nigga locked up on some bullshit."

I was glad when he brushed past Momma to grab his coat from the closet by the door.

"No, Roy, don't go," my momma said, turning to hold his arm and take his coat out his hand. "I'll take care of this," she told him.

She grabbed my arm and pulled me like a rag doll into my room. I didn't even cry as she spanked me with one of my own shoes. I lay

*on the floor on my side. She squatted down
beside me and I could smell the stank of her
crotch. "Now you stop your damn lies. Roy is
good to me and you. I'm not gone let you run
off a good man who help pay these bills
around here. I need Roy. I love him. I ain't
gone let you fuck this up for me."*

*She left me, her six-year-old daughter, her
Princess, right on that floor and went to that
man she needed and loved so much.*

*A little piece of me died right then and
there.*

My momma ain't shit. Period.

I'm older now and I am sick and tired of any and
every one of *her* men feeling me and fucking me
when they get ready. I will be eighteen soon. Legally
an adult. A woman. Old enough to vote. Well, my
vote is for *her* men to stay the fuck away from me.

I glance at the little Betty Boop clock my granny
gave me when I was six or so. It's going on 1:00 p.m. I
got to hustle. Momma will leave by one to catch the
bus to get to her night shift at the Super Wal-Mart. I
will be up out this piece right along with her.

I got up and threw on a pair of no-name jeans and
a pink T-shirt with Princess written across the chest in

rhinestones. Both are straight out of Wal-Mart. *Humph*. I ain't even know what owning designer clothes is. If it wasn't for the clothes Lucky either gave me or let me borrow, I would really be a joke at North Atlanta High.

I can have plenty of Baby Phat, Juicy Couture, and everything else if my momma would spend my child support on me and not taking care of these little boys pretending to be men.

I'm sitting on the edge of my lumpy twin bed pulling on my sneakers when a mouse crawls out of its hole big and bold like he pay rent. I don't even bother to chase it away. Shit, I couldn't outrun no rat. Besides, let his ass battle the roaches for this shit hole 'cause I ain't give a damn about this room nor the raggedy-ass apartment it's in.

I make my bed quick and look around my room to make sure the few items I have are in a place—if not in its place. Hard to make a raggedy-ass, broke-down end table have its own right place in a damn bedroom.

I open my bedroom door and listen. I could hear my momma up and about in her bedroom. It's still early for Cash so he probably sleeping—sitting around the house all day makes his drop-shot ass real tired. Please.

I cross the hall and open the bathroom door. I jump back to find Cash already in there naked as he stands over the toilet pissing. He strokes his dick. My eyes jerk up to his face.

That sick bitch has the nerve to smile at me.

I slam the door back close and cross the narrow hall back to my room to slam that door, too. I grab my journal from one of my hiding spots.

> *Why can't it be just me and my momma? Why ain't I enough for her? She always gots to have some man living here. Always. Don't none of them love her 'cause they wouldn't be bothering me or hitting on her and cheating on her. Cash ain't gone be no better. Just watch.*

There's a knock at my door. My heart pounds and I feel so afraid. Kenny, one of my momma's exes, would always knock all polite and shit before he would open the door and come right on in the room to get in my bed with me while my momma slept. I was only eight. I WAS ONLY EIGHT! Way too young for a grown man to put his thing in my mouth.

Pain hit me in the chest and I force myself to breathe slow and deep. I taught myself how to calm down so this shit—the memories—doesn't get to me so bad but I know I'm just digging a hole deeper in my soul to bury all that shit.

"I'm out the bathroom," Cash says through the door before I hear him laugh.

I don't move until I hear him walk down the hall and close the bedroom door.

I wipe my sweaty palms on my jeans before I pick up my pen.

> *He think he doing something strutting around here like a broke pimp. How can a broke nigga like him have a name like Cash? Just fucking stupid as hell. If he knew how many men done walk around here like they the king to Queen he would get that big Kool-Aid grin off his face. So many men done slept in that same bed, in that same room, in this same apartment.*

I close my journal and put it back in my closet in the inner pocket of this old pleather coat I don't wear no more. I head to the bathroom and rush through brushing my teeth and washing my face. In the mirror I look at my face.

People always tell me I'm pretty.

"You look like LaLa from MTV."

"Your hazel eyes so pretty."

"Is that reddish brown your real hair color?"

"Is that all your hair?"

When I think of all the hands and shit on me through the years, I wish I had another face. Maybe they woulda left me alone. I look away from the mirror and leave the bathroom to walk to their bedroom door.

"Harder. Fuck me harder, Daddy," my mother moans.

"Damn, this pussy good," Cash says with a grunt.

I feel nauseous at their sex sounds. "Ma, I'm going to Lucky's," I call out. I turn and walk so fast down that hall that I think my feet gone make fire or some shit.

Leaving the apartment always makes me feel better. Free. Each step takes weight off my shoulders. Each step makes me feel better. Down the hall and the pissy stairwell. Out the door. Away from my momma. Away from the memories and the misery. So goddamned free.

"Hey, Princess."

I look up at Lucky waving down to me from her bedroom window.

"I was just about to call you. Come up. I gotta surprise for you."

The whole time I'm headed up the stairwell I'm wondering what Lucky's crazy ass is up to. With her *anything* is possible.

Before I can even knock she opens the front door. "What's up—"

My eyes land on Dean and some dude I don't know lounging on the leather sofa in the living room. Lucky puts a hand to my back to push me forward. My feet feel like they're glued to the damn floor. I already smell a hookup and I ain't want no part of it.

"Princess, this Dean's cousin Ahmaad." Lucky grabs my hand and pulls me into the living room behind her. "Ahmaad, this is my best friend, Princess."

Okay. He's cute. Dark chocolate skin. Fresh cornrows. Bright eyes. Long-ass lashes. Good mouth. Dimpled chin. He smiles up at me and I have to admit that he has a nice one.

"Y'all come and sit down," Dean says. The boys move farther down onto opposite ends of the couch to make room.

I'm going to plant my size nine in Lucky's hot ass.

As soon as we sit down Lucky damn near climbs into Dean's lap. Ahmaad and I look at each other all awkward and shit as they start moaning and groaning as they kiss each other.

Okay, this ain't my type of party.

Lucky rises to her feet as she pulls Dean behind her. "Y'all go 'head and chill. Get to know each other and all that good shit. We'll be right back."

Dean laughs as he watches the movement of her body as they walk away.

My mouth drops open. "Lucky. Luc-ky," I call out.

I watch as her bedroom door closes behind them. I jump right down on the other end of the couch. It's quiet as hell, so I reach for the remote to turn on the television.

"You go to school with Lucky, right?" he asks.

I look at him out the corner of my eye as I nod. Right then I can imagine how the hell an asthma attack feels. It's so hard for me to sit on this sofa while my best friend is sexing her man in the next room. I want to run but I don't. I want to be a normal teen, able to flirt and kiss and let a boy cop a feel . . . but I can't. I just can't.

He scoots his ass down closer to me on the sofa and I swallow over a cookie-size lump in my throat. "Don't be scared," he says to me as the scent of his cologne gets a little stronger.

His hand touches my thigh.

Faces come flashing back to me. Way too many faces of men who have flittered in and out of my life over the years. Fucked-up men who made me feel fucked up. I'm so nauseous. My heart pounds at the memories.

"You're so pretty," he whispers near my ear.

I shiver all over in disgust.

"Motherfucker, don't touch me," I say to him real soft but real damn firm.

Ahmaad looks real confused. "Huh?"

I jump to my feet. "Don't fucking touch me," I yell at him . . . at all the men haunting my damn memories.

Lucky's door opens. She has one arm over her naked breasts as she comes running out to us still wearing her jeans. Dean follows with his dick hanging between his thighs before he jerks up his pants. "What's going on?" they ask, looking at me like I'm crazy as hell.

Even though Ahmaad didn't really do shit wrong, I am afraid.

Even though I know I didn't do nothing wrong, I am ashamed.

Even though I know Lucky meant well, I am angry.

I wrap my arms around myself as I let out a deep breath. I feel like a damn weirdo or some shit.

"Shit, all I did was tell her psycho ass she pretty and touch her leg," Ahmaad says in his defense, like somebody accused his ass of rape or some shit. He jumps up from the couch and walks over to stand by Dean.

I cover my face with my hands and drop down to sit on the couch. Maybe I am psycho.

Lucky comes over to me and sits down. I feel her hand on my back and for some reason it makes the tears fall from my eyes. "Damn, Lucky . . . I hate my fucking life," I admit to her in a whisper.

"Man, that bitch crazy," Ahmaad says with a suck of his teeth. "*This* what the fuck y'all call me over here for?"

"Damn, Lucky, why your girl trippin'?" Dean asks. "She don't want no dick and then she gone block you from gettin' some."

"Get out," Lucky says instantly as she jumps to her feet.

I look up as Lucky pushes both of them out the front door with her titties swinging like fists.

"Lucky, send her ass home," Dean complains, obviously angry.

"Fuck that. I'm sending *y'all* home." Lucky opens the front door before she covers her breasts with her arms again. "Y'all niggas ain't gone sit up in this bitch and talk shit 'bout my friend. And then y'all don't even know what the fuck y'all talkin' 'bout. Get ghost, motherfuckers!"

Dean gives Lucky a pleading look.

"I'll call you later. Bye. Damn."

She slams the door and walks into her bedroom. When she comes back out she has on her T-shirt. She drops down onto the couch beside me.

"I'm sorry, Lucky—"

She smiles at me even though her eyes are as sad as my soul. "No, I'm sorry. I was so busy trying to find you a boyfriend that I actually forgot all the shit you told me. My dumb ass wasn't thinking that sex and boys don't mean the same to you because of . . ."

We fall silent. The words "molestation," "sexual abuse," and "rape" are there in the air between us even if we don't say them.

No one but Lucky knows my story. She is the keeper of my secrets.

I drop my head as pain pierces me. "What about Dean?" I ask.

Lucky reaches over to offer me her fist. "Fuck him, 'cause right now you need me way more than his dick does."

It feels so good to have somebody I can rely on. I make a fist and tap it against the top of hers.

8

Woo Woo

One Month Later

"I love you. Damn, I love you."

I shiver like crazy as my husband wraps his arms around me tight as hell and strokes deep inside of me. His lips cover mine and I give him my tongue to suck as I shift my hands down to grip his ass. I bring my legs up to wrap around his waist as his strokes deepen until I feel like his dick is going to split me.

I quiver beneath him on our bed as my nut rises and builds. I suck his tongue harder before I gasp as I feel my juices squirt out and coat every inch of him. Those spasms have my ass trembling as I spread my legs open and give in to the sensation. Shit. It feels good.

"Damn right," he whispers in my ear as he shifts his hands to lean up and spread my legs wider.

His pumps come faster and harder like a fucking machine until the moment his dick pumps like a gun and fills me with his seed. Shit, he can hardly move as he cums. It's like his ass is having a stroke or something.

I work my hips and my sugar walls to finish pulling the last of his nut from him as I deeply lick and bite his nipples just the way he loves.

Reggie rolls over onto his back breathing hard and I roll over with him to lie against his side. "Hey," I say softly, tilting my head back to look at him.

He opens one eye. "Yeah, baby?"

"I love you, Reggie," I tell him with emotion as I look up into his handsome square face.

"I love you, too." He playfully slaps my ass.

I lay there stroking his chest until his snores cause my hand to tremble. Knowing he's asleep, I ease out of bed and head for the bathroom. As soon as I close the door, I lock it and pull on my housecoat from the back of the door.

After a good meal and a good fuck I like to blow me a blunt. Fuck it. It rests my nerves.

I open the window next to the tub, pulling back the curtain. Thank God for the hedges between our house and our neighbor's or Mr. Wilson's old wrinkled white ass would get a helluva peep show on a daily basis.

I reach for my makeup bag and dig down to the bottom for the empty lipstick case holding my Life-savers . . . three blunts. It's Hawaiian marijuana wrapped in cherry-flavored blunts—my favorite blend.

I pull up the stool from my dressing table in the corner and sit with my head stuck out the window. I make sure to blow that thick-ass smoke out into the wind.

Reggie and I met at his small dental practice in Buckhead. I was his front-desk receptionist. First we started chitchatting during downtimes at the office, but somehow I started feeling this straitlaced cat with the glasses. Probably what was even more shot out was that his goody-two-shoes ass started feeling me, too.

I blow another stream of smoke out the window.

To everybody's surprise in the office we started to go out on dates. Shit, my ass ain't never *dated* nobody. Either I was fucking some dude just to get the pressure off or I had somebody who was my man straight up. I ain't know shit about the in-between.

He taught me shit and I taught him a few things. His lessons were usually outside the bedroom. Mine wasn't. Fuck it. I'm good at what I do and I *always* make it do what it do, baby.

Reggie ain't even know my ass still smoke weed on the regular. Shit, there's a lot he doesn't know about me.

Like Hassan.

But that is over. I haven't spoken to him since that night before my wedding. That was the last time I would give in to my fixation on that Negro. No matter how many times Hassan calls my cell phone and sets off the ringtone I didn't answer. I haven't been back to Bentley Manor or any part of that side of town since. I checks in with my peeps via the phone but I'm not going back. Temptation is a bitch I'm trying to avoid.

In time I will forget the way Hassan makes me feel. In time I will be able to say "Fuck him." In time this new life of mine—that doesn't include Hassan— will fit me just fine.

I done went from Bankhead to Buckhead. From a $9.00/hour job to being a housewife. From low-rent apartments to a four-bedroom home with a game room, an office, and a pool. From being a certified ghetto chick to a suburban lady.

But I miss the hood. For me "so ghetto is so good."

These damn suburbs is boring as shit and I'm getting just as humdrum as our neighbors. I ain't had nobody to gossip with—and God knows I used to live to keep up on *everybody's* business in Bentley Manor. Me and them old chicks Cleo and Osceola used to straight battle for the gossip crown. Nobody to hang out and chill with. Nobody to blaze with. Man, what the fuck?

I hold the blunt out the window and look over my shoulder at my reflection in the large mirror over the sink. I don't look like my damn self no more. Who is that woman in the mirror, 'cause it damn sure ain't look like WooWoo.

Once Reggie proposed and offered for me to move into his house, I began to really notice how different we were. Living with someone will really let you in on the realness.

For my wedding I had my signature braids removed and wore my own shoulder-length hair in this pretty-ass rod set. I decided to take off the bright neon airbrush designs on my nails for a simpler pink and white French manicure. My makeup was more laid back than the eye shadow I wore that always . . . *always* matched my gear. Oh, a sister used to stay *coordinated.*

For Reggie it was a different WooWoo standing at the altar with him. And although he always said he loved my wild and crazy clothes, my braids, and my matchy-matchy style, he saw something at that altar that his laid-back ass liked more. Shit.

When we on our honeymoon in Negril, Jamaica, Reggie admitted to me that he preferred my new hair, nails, and makeup. Mind you, my ass had already made an appointment with my beautician and my nail tech to get my shit back right the *very* day we got back to A-T-L.

Wanting to please my husband and to fit in with my new environment, I canceled the waist-length braids and crazy nails and cut back on the makeup . . . for now. My marriage is new and I want it to work. Reggie's real good to me and I want to be a good wife to him. So far so good.

The doorknob rattles. I take one last drag off the blunt before I jump off the stool and toss the last of it into the toilet. It hisses as it hits the water.

"Leesha . . . why you lock the door?"

I roll my eyes heavenward as I shut the window. Quick as can be I drink some mouthwash. I nearly gag as some of it goes down my throat.

"I'm coming," I holler before I flush the toilet again.

I spray air freshener as I walk to the door and un-lock it.

"You a'ight?" he asks as he moves past me.

As I walk out, I turn and watch him take a long-ass piss.

"I'm cool," I lie, just wanting his ass out of that bathroom before he picks up on the smell of the weed. *Damn, go to bed,* I'm thinking as I drop my robe and climb into our king-sized bed. I keep my eyes on his ass until he flushes the toilet, turns off the bathroom light, and comes back to bed.

Even as we settle back down for the night, I lie there with my eyes closed thinking it is way too quiet in the burbs.

"Excuse me, baby, I'll be right back." We are standing in the parking lot of Reverend Yarborough's megachurch God's Temple chatting with Reggie's mother, Ella, before the televised church services.

They both excuse me and I walk inside the massive and sadditified church to head to the bathroom. I wish like hell that I could rip off these stockings, but I already learned the hard way that his mother wouldn't approve. Not wanting another etiquette lesson I'd just have to suffer. They always make my legs itch.

In the stall I squat over the commode. Five-million-dollar church or not, I ain't trying to pick up shit nobody gots to give.

Bzzzzzzzzzz.

That's my cell phone vibrating in my purse. I finish up and flush before I reach for it. My heart swells the fuck up at the sight of Hassan's number.

Bzzzzzzzzzz.

I pull my black Ann Taylor skirt back down and drop down on the toilet seat as the phone continues to vibrate in my hand.

Bzzzzzzzzzz.

I want to answer that phone so bad. I want to be with him so bad. I want to fuck him so bad.

Bzzzzzzzzzz.

But being with Hassan is bad for me for so many reasons. So many fucked-up reasons that I can't change. Not just his nasty-ass temper or slinging dope—those he can fix. There is shit I can't accept. Shit I can't change. Still, that doesn't make my ass want him or crave him or need him any less.

Bzzzzzzzzzz.

Not once during the last month did this motherfucker give up trying to reach me. I can hear the hurt and betrayal in his messages because I went ahead and married Reggie. He feels used, and to be honest, I did take advantage of him that last night. I used him up for all the memories I would need to last me a lifetime.

Bzzzzzzzzzzz.

My bottom lip quivers and I bite it as I look down at my phone. Tears fill my eyes as I press the vibrating phone against my face. I almost fool myself into imagining it's Hassan's hands on me.

"Hassan baby, I miss you," I whisper aloud inside the stall.

Bzzzzzzzzzzz.

I let my head drop back as I push my breasts forward and spread my legs wide. My heart races and I feel real emotional. Real conflicted. Confused.

Bzzzzzzzzzzz.

Hassan has to be hanging up and calling back. Each buzz lets me know that he ain't gave up on me. On us. Even though I have to leave him alone that shit makes me feel good.

Bzzzzzzzzzzz.

My breath starts coming faster and that stall gets hot as hell. My nipples ache as they rub against my gold silk Donna Karan shirt. I swallow hard and let my tears fall as I pull my panties to the side to tear a hole in the seat of the stockings, then push my pulsating cell phone down against my throbbing clit.

Bzzzzzzzzzzz.

"Ah," I gasp, biting my bottom lip as I think of Hassan. His hands. His lips. His tongue. The feel of his body. The taste of his mouth. The taste of his body. Just being in his fucking arms. In his bed. In his life.

Bzzzzzzzzzzz.

The vibrations of the phone against my clit is nothing compared to the feel of Hassan's hand but at that moment just knowing it's him calling is enough to make me lift my legs and press my feet against each wall of the bathroom stall. My face twists in a mix of torture and pleasure as I circle the phone against my clit until my pussy starts smacking it up from its juices.

Bzzzzzzzzzzz.

My hips jerk as I cum. I have to drop one foot to the floor to keep from falling off the toilet. "Hassan," I moan as I raise a hand to squeeze one of my nipples through my shirt.

Bzzzzzzzzzzz.

"Ah . . . ah . . . ah," I grunt hoarsely as I let the tears fall.

My body goes slack and I drop my shiny wet phone to the floor as I wipe the tears from my face. I just know my makeup is jacked. I'll have to straighten it up before I go up to face my husband and my prim and proper mother-in-law. No need for them to know that I just damn near cheated on my husband *inside* the church. I'll probably go to hell.

Fuck it.

I'm learning that living without Hassan is its own kind of goddamn hell.

9

Takiah

"Repent: for the kingdom of heaven is at hand," Pastor Eddie Meyer roars from the Missionary Baptist church pulpit, mopping his sweaty forehead with his ever-present white handkerchief. His fevered gaze sweeps across the small congregation, and then stops and settles on me.

Why am I surprised?

While doing his thing, Pastor Meyer looks more like a raving pit bull with round frog-shaped eyes, a gray and white horseshoe hairline, and jiggling jowls that puts me in the mood for puddin' pops.

Attractive, he's not.

I feel joy, fear, and an overwhelming sense of nausea all at the same time. Shit. I need to pull myself together.

"You may think it's too late for you," he continues, pointin' a trembling finger. "Well, I'm here to tell you it's not. As long as there's breath in your body, the war for your soul rages on."

Tears swell in my eyes and despite our locked gazes, I know he can't possibly be talkin' about me. He doesn't know about *all* the things I've done. The drugs. The men. The crimes.

Even now as I sit next to my grandmother in the middle of Sunday's church service, I want a hit so bad I can taste it. When I leave here I'll probably score a G-rock from Hassan—probably offer him some pussy instead of cash. Does that sound like someone whose soul can be saved?

"What young people have to realize is that their bodies and spirits belong to God."

"Amen," someone cosigns.

"Your *soul* belongs to Him. Obey and He will give you what your soul wants and needs."

"Hallelujah," someone else shouts.

I swallow hard and blink back my burning tears. A part of me wants to believe the old pastor. How silly is that? I grew up in this matchbox church and know most of these people come just to be seen, not to be saved. None of these hypocrites ever fooled me: Wife beaters, child abusers, drug dealers, dogs, and hos are all sitting together and riding the fast train to hell.

"Proverbs 13:15 tells us: Good understanding giveth favor, but the way of the transgressor is hard," Pastor Meyer rants, dabbing his white hankie along his double chin. "Put down those drugs and start focusing on establishing a relationship with our heavenly father. It doesn't matter how much crack you smoked or how your man pimped you out. It doesn't matter how much drugs you did while you were pregnant. God is waiting on you!"

No, this Negro didn't.

I glance to my left and then to my right. Sure enough, more than half these hypocritical bastards' eyes are on me. It takes everything I have not to flash these assholes the bird or flip up my dress and tell them all to kiss my ass. Pastor Eddie Meyer included. Him and his holier-than-thou sermons.

Look at him. Standing up there like he's Jesus Christ himself and waving his damn finger like I'm his damn child or something.

Tanana stirs in my arms, probably because my leg is bouncing like an out-of-control jackhammer. See, I knew it was a mistake to come to this motherfucker.

Grandma Cleo places a hand on my knee and I obligingly stop bouncing it. When I glance at her, she stares calm, cool, and collected at Pastor Meyer like she didn't just hear his ass put all my business out on Front Street.

And guess what. I can't do jack shit but sit here and take it. For a brief and insane moment, I think I was better off in D.C.

Now I know I'm trippin'.

I'm a dead woman if Kameron ever gets his hands on me. Not only did I fuck up his money, but I torched his GQ-face pretty good during our last fight. Of course, it was self-defense, seeing how he was busy trying to choke the shit out of me.

Just thinking back on that fight has me fightin' tears—and not because of what you may think. I sort of miss that son of a bitch. How sick is that?

I forget my anger at the good pastor and allow my thoughts to tumble back through time. . . .

"Goddammit, T," Kameron shouted, storming butt-naked out of our bedroom; his black dick swinging fiercely between his legs. "Can't you shut that damn baby up?"

"Yeah. Yeah. In a minute," I promised, breaking a piece of a Brillo pad and placing it in my glass pipe. "Let me just get a hit to calm my nerves," I said. Tanana had been crying

all damn day and if I don't hit this shit I just knew I was gone toss her out a window or something.

This momma shit was harder than I thought. Feedings, shitty diapers, crying, and then the whole thing starts all over again. Hell, I don't know why I always had to do everything. He was her daddy . . . probably. It wouldn't hurt him to pitch in every once in a while while I rest a bit.

"Hell, naw." Kameron stomped his way over piles of clothes and junk in the middle of the living room and snatched the pipe from my fingers.

"Fuck. Give me that back," I snapped.

"Naw, pimpin'. You hit this and all you're gonna do is lie around and sleep. Go see about the baby."

I jump to my feet and try to grab the pipe back. "She's fine. It ain't gonna kill her to cry every once in a while. If you're so damn worried about her, you go check on her!" I never saw the slap, but it literally launched my ass into the air. When my head banged against the wall, no shit, I felt like one of those Saturday morning cartoons where bright yellow stars circled my head and the sound of tweeting birds filled the room.

"Your mouth is gettin' out of hand. When I tell your ass to do somethin', I don't want no damn lip," he raged.

My heart rattles around my rib cage as I try to push myself up off the floor. It's no use. My damn legs won't work.

"Whoa, guys." Lena, Kameron's latest and greatest ho, raced her naked ass into the living room with Tanana screaming on her hip. "It's okay. I got her. I think she just needs a bottle."

The sight of this trick with my baby enraged the fuck out me. "What the hell do you think you're doing?" I snapped.

"Shut the fuck up and get up," Kameron snarled. The glassy fury in his eyes made it clear that he was as high as I wanted to be right now; of course, he was sniffing the good stuff, while I'm strung out on this cheap-ass crack. This was just his way of punishing me 'cause I'd refused to go back out on the street since having the baby. And according to him, this decision was hurting business.

As if.

Sure, I had a rep for giving the best damn

head and pussy this side of D.C.; but damn, I was sick of this shit. I'm his wife, goddammit.

"I said get the fuck up!" Kameron snatched a handful of my matted weave and yanked me to my feet.

"Ow," was all I can manage to say.

"You need to fall back in line. Ever since you had this damn baby, all you do is lie around and smoke up my shit. You think I'm runnin' some kind of charity? This shit ain't free."

Truth be told, I couldn't concentrate on what he was saying. The pain in my head was fuckin' killin' me and all I'm tryna do is get him to release his grip. Instead, I made a real error in judgment and swung my acrylic nails toward Kameron's eyes.

"Bitch!"

I'd never dreamed of an ass-whuppin' like this. Sure, Kameron had slapped me around before, but this time, the sheer power and the wild, almost crazed way his fists pounded against my gut and chest, I was convinced I'd die from the pain before internal bleeding. I just wanted the pain to stop. That's all I re-membered thinking. I grabbed a bottle of 151 on the table and smashed it on his head. He grunted, his grip slackened a bit, but he didn't release me. Not until after I reached for the lighter next to my pipe and lit his ass up. Next thing I knew that motherfucker was a ball of fire. . . .

"Let us bow our heads and pray," Pastor Meyer instructs and his herd of sheep obeys, although not every eye closes.

"O Lord, we come humble before you and ask for your guidance, for wisdom and courage. As you've promised, we know all things done outside of Christ will be tossed into the sea of forgetfulness. Only people inside of Christ's saving grace will survive. If there is any among us who are still enslaved to the pleasures of the flesh, touch their heart, O Lord, and let them see that you are the way and the light. For these things we pray, Amen."

A hundred unsynchronized "Amens" end the prayer and before you know it, it's over.

"Thank God Almighty. We're free at last," I mumble under my breath. Judging by the murderous look in my grandma's eyes, it isn't quiet enough. "Sorry," I say, feeling like an errant toddler. Grandma Cleo has that way about her, whether you are her child or not.

"Learn anything?" Miz Nosceola asks from my right.

Seriously, this old bitch gets on my nerves. "Only that the more things change, the more they stay the same," I answer.

"Amen, chile." Her eyes rake over me. "Amen."

Fuck her.

Outside, I'm tryin' not to feel like the freak of nature I am, wearing a floral dress Grandma Cleo retrieved from the back of her closet that obviously hadn't seen the light of day since the late eighties and wearing flat, too-white shoes that just screamed Pay-Less. At least I had a new pink sweater that covered the tracks and tattoos on my arms.

"I sure hope you enjoyed today's service," Pastor Meyer says, sneaking up behind me.

When I turn to face him, prepared to let him know just how unimpressed I truly was, Grandma Cleo butts her nose into the conversation before I can fire off a comment that will embarrass her.

"Absolutely wonderful, Pastor." Her smile beams.

"And timely, too," Miz Osceola chirps. "We can't wait to hear this evening's service as well."

Damn. Here we go. Now I'm supposed to come back for another service? Why is it that black folks want to stay up in church *all* day?

Pastor Meyer smiles and his inky black eyes actually sparkle as if he hears my thoughts. "Perhaps it's a bit too much to ask that Ms. Takiah and Tanana take in two services on their first day back to church?"

Again I open my mouth to answer, but Grandma Cleo is right there, actin' like I've gone mute or something.

"Don't be silly. They would love to come back this evening. Ain't that right, Takiah?"

All eyes, including my baby's, zero in on me. What the hell am I supposed to say? I'd put off coming here for over a month. There are only so many excuses a religious grandma is going to put up with from a freeloading, crack-addicted granddaughter.

Grandma Cleo is on a mission to save my soul whether I want her to or not.

"I understand," Pastor Meyer says, still smiling patiently. "These things take time." He captures my hand. "We just want you to know that the Lord is here for you, whenever you're ready."

I nod, fighting the urge to yank my hand back; then I see my grandma give him a little elbow. Lord Jesus, what now?

Pastor Meyer looks at Grandma Cleo and then clears his throat. "Takiah, from time to time it comes to my attention that *some* members of my congregation are in need of a little extra . . . help on their path to enlightenment."

My eyes cut to Grandma. "Oh, really?"

"Yes." He nods, obviously encouraged by my lack of protest. "I'm more than willing to meet with you for further counseling—to help you conquer your addictions. One on one."

I don't respond. Trust me. It's the right thing to do, since my impulse is to cuss them all out for this mini intervention right in front of the church's door when there are still groups of nosy busybodies crowdin' our space and eavesdroppin'.

"Just think about it," he says, finally sensing the storm brewin' up inside of me.

"She will," Grandma Cleo answers, and then flashes me a look. "Won't you, Takiah?"

I just turn and walk away.

The nerve.

10

Keisha

This beauty school shit is kickin' my ass.

Seriously, it's not at all what I expected and just about everything I hoped it wouldn't be. Books, readin', studyin', and tests—I thought hair schools just handed you a bunch of mannequin heads and let you do your thang. Now I have to learn about different hair textures, how to spot and repair damaged hair. All of this while havin' to deal with Jasmine's strep throat, Jordan tryna fight everybody who calls his dad a crackhead, Jada's ear infection, and Jackson's bed-wetting.

I mean, what the fuck? Do I wear a costume with a giant *S* printed on the front or something?

And if that's not enough, I have Smokey startin' in on me just about every night.

"It's about damn time," Smokey growls the moment I usher the kids inside the door. He looks at his wrist like he has a watch, knowing damn well he hocked that son of a bitch a long time ago.

"Class ran late," I tell him, slammin' the door behind me as a hint that I'm not in the mood for any bullshit. He's huddled on the floor where our pleather couch used to be. I don't even have the strength to ask what happened to it.

"This is bullshit," Smokey mumbles under his breath, and then spots the happy meal boxes the kids are carryin'. "Fuck. What about me? What the hell am I supposed to eat?"

"Shakespeare bought it for them." I toss him the rumpled bag in my hand that contains his Big Mac and fries. "We didn't forget you." I turn to the kids. "Y'all get ready to take your baths."

Without a "hello" or "how you doin'" to their daddy, the kids shuffle off to their bedrooms. I, on the other hand, turn to face him. "You fell off the wagon again." It is a question as much as a statement and to be honest, I don't know why I even bother sayin' anything.

Instead of respondin', Smokey chomps down on his burger like it's the best thing he's ever tasted. During his moanin' and smackin', I frown and feel a wave of disgust crash through every pore of my body. In his rank clothes, nasty braids, and nappy facial hair, my husband looks more like an animal than a man.

I watch and wait for that maternal instinct I've held on to for so long to hit me, but even that's elusive to me tonight.

"What the hell are you looking at?" Smokey growls. He looks up at me, a few smeared drops of mayonnaise and catsup cling to his wiry facial hair.

"Nothing," I mumble under my breath and drop my gaze. My eyes burn like I've poured battery acid on them or something. Why couldn't he beat this?

I did.

"You think you're better than me, don't you?"

At the biting accusation, my eyes snap back up to meet his. I don't answer because . . . I do think I'm better. I've been clean for four years and it's just through the grace of God that my children show no effects of my idiotic drug past.

Smokey grows impatient through my silence and snarls out a, "You're not."

"I didn't say—"

"You were thinking it," he shouts.

I clamp my jaw shut. Already during our short,

heated exchange, my exhaustion has doubled. I already know where this is going and I don't want to take it there.

"I told Shakespeare dat dis school shit was a mistake. You already doin' folks' hair. What the fuck you need a license fo?"

"I already told you . . . so I can open my own shop."

"That's just some more bullshit." He crams the rest of his burger down his throat and then backhands his mouth and face clean—as clean as possible, anyway.

Instead of letting it drop, like I shoulda, I defend the small seeds of hope Shakespeare has planted in me. "It's not bullshit."

In case you didn't know, crackheads are quick. Smokey is off the floor so fast, it may be possible he flew.

"You ain't foolin' nobody, Keisha," he says, giving me a faceful of spit. "You tryna go to school like Shakespeare so you can leave my ass stuck in this hellhole."

"That's not true," I lie unconvincingly.

He shakes his head, his eyes more than glossy just from his drug-induced high. "You would leave me, wouldn't you?"

He searches my face, my eyes and, instead riskin' gettin' caught in another lie, I remain quiet.

The blow from his open palm stuns me, and before I can recover I receive another slap that jars my face in the opposite direction. "You ain't goin' no goddamn where. You got that?" He's shouting so loud my eardrum threatens to bust.

Not waiting for my head to clear, I strike out at him. My hands and nails sink into his tough, dry skin, but Smokey's drug of choice gives him Superman-like strength and his hand wraps around my throat and literally lifts me off the floor.

"You hear me, Keisha? I'll fuckin' kill you before I let you leave me in this bitch!"

The next thing I hear is Jasmine's multi-octave scream. It, along with my lack of oxygen, causes my head to explode with pain. Another scream, and then another. My babies are all filled with the terror that Daddy is gonna kill Momma.

Baby, it's okay, I want to tell them, but the lie is stuck inside my head since Smokey is determined to crush my neck. I kick and claw at a hand that feels more like steel with every passin' second.

It's no use.

This is it.

This is the night my husband is gonna kill me and what's worse, he's gonna do it right here in front of my babies.

✧   ✦   ✧

When I come to, I'm surrounded by white people. This may be no big deal to some but where I'm from it can only mean one thing: somebody had called the police.

I try to move.

"Hold on." A gruff, redneck-looking motherfucker restrains me and then asks, "Can you tell me your name?"

"What kind of crazy question is that?" I try to sit up, but again was held down. "Will you get the fuck off me?"

The man's jaw hardens like he's ready to give me directions on how to kiss his ass, but he maintains control of himself.

"Ma'am. I just need to make sure you're all right or if we need to take you down to Grady."

"Grady?" I blink. "I don't need to go to no damn hospital. I'm fine." I finally manage to shove him off of me and win my freedom to sit up. "Where are my babies?"

"Downstairs with your neighbor, Miz Cleo." A mousy brunette squats next to the redneck. "Where they usually are," she adds. "And your husband has been taken downtown to cool his heels behind bars— again."

For the first time I recognize her bony ass. She's been called out to my apartment a few times before. The look in her dull blue eyes isn't sympathy, and I find myself barkin' the same words from Smokey to her. "You think you're better than me, don't you?"

She ignores the question and finishes packin' up her stuff. When she stands and turns toward the door, I still can't let it go. "I asked you a question," I shout at her back.

Her cold eyes pierce me. To my relief she still refuses to answer the question.

"Honey chile. Are you sure you're all right?" Miz Cleo asks the moment she ushers me into her apartment. My eyes mist as I look around and note how much her place looks more like a home than the one I provide for my kids.

"Yeah," I rasp, despite my sore throat.

My children, along with Miz Cleo's granddaughter, Takiah, are huddled around the dining room table in their pajamas and digging through their separate bowls of ice cream. I feel like an ass because I been meanin' to come over and say hey to the girl. I remember her being sort of fast and a little bit of a troublemaker when she was a teenager, and judging by the tracks in her arms that she was trying to hide, nothing has changed.

We exchange awkward "hellos" and then I feel like a gigantic ass tryna pull my children away from their frozen desserts. "C'mon, y'all. We gotta go home."

"You know," Miz Cleo says, undoubtedly touched by the children's frowns. "They are more than welcome to stay here tonight. I have a couple of extra beds they can share if you need a little time for yourself."

"Thank you for the offer, but—"

"Please, Mommy. Can we stay?" Jasmine launches into a heartfelt campaign. "I promise we'll be good."

"Jasmine, Miz Cleo already has . . . " My eyes inadvertently slide toward Takiah. "Company."

"Oh, hush, chile," Miz Cleo says, wrapping a protective arm around me. "There's plenty of room. Don't forget, I raised my own four in this place. As long as they don't mind sharing two to a bed, we're all gonna get along just fine."

My babies jump down from the table and surround me in a bouncing circle.

"Please, Mommy. Please?"

I don't know why, but my kids love them some Miz Cleo. Despite their hopeful faces, I still want to say no, because that would mean I'd be alone in our apartment. I don't like being alone.

I never have.

"I don't mind," Miz Cleo says, hugging me.

"Well . . . all right," I say, giving in.

The children explode with a collective "Yay!" and Takiah quickly reminds them not to wake her baby. Damn, I'd forgotten that Takiah came back with a baby.

"Miz Cleo, maybe—"

"It's all right," she assures while directing me toward the door. "You get you some rest," she insists, and then adds for my ears only, "I've been wantna tell you how proud I am to see you goin' to school."

I literally blush from the praise. "Thanks. Shakespeare, uh, sort of put the idea in my head."

"Well, good for him. I'm proud of him, too. He didn't let this place swallow him whole. I'm just prayin' that you follow his example and stop tryna save everybody instead of yourself."

Her speech hits me as being hypocritical, but she seems to read my mind. "I speak from experience." She winks and gives my waist another hug. "Get you some rest and think about what I said."

I return to my quiet apartment. Tears brim my eyes before I even shut the door good. I hate this place. I hate my life. For these reasons, I know I'm not gonna give up school. No matter how hard it is.

Before today, I was content to die in this place. Now the thought scares the hell out of me. To the point I don't even want to stay here tonight.

Not alone.

I hate being alone.

Shakespeare doesn't believe his eyes when he opens the door to his modest brick ranch house on the Gwinnett County line. "Keesh?" he asks, digging the sleep out the corners of his eyes and then glancing out to the street behind me. "What's up? Somethin' happened to Smokey?"

Fear interlaces his concern and I instantly know how he feels. How many days have I waited for the ultimate bad news?

"No. Well . . . he's in jail."

Shakespeare's searching gaze traveled no farther than my bruised neck before he exhales a long breath and steps back from the door.

"What happened?" he asks, once I close the door.

"The usual," I answer, and then remember the mousy brunette with the cold blue eyes. "He doesn't like me going to school."

Drawing in a deep breath, Shakespeare shakes his head because there's really nothing to say. Didn't we both expect this?

"I'm not going to quit," I tell him.

Our eyes meet and somethin' passes between us. Somethin' that makes me smile.

"You look like you could use a drink."

No. I want you to hold me and tell me that everything is gonna be fine. "I'll take a bottle of whateva you got."

Nodding, he turns and I follow him to the living room. While he walks, my gaze drinks in his strong profile and it's quite a sight, since he's only wearing a pair of black boxers. Muscles ripple beneath his smooth maple-brown skin and I swear to God I wish I had a purse full of quarters to see if I can bounce them off his firm ass.

I realize what I'm thinkin' and at the same moment Shakespeare turns to me.

"I can make you a—what's wrong?"

"Nothing," I lie, wide-eyed.

He cocks his head like an adorable puppy and stares. "Are you sure? You can tell me."

I can't help but laugh. "Nothing. I think I can really use that drink right about now."

He stares at me for a moment longer and then

turns toward his box-cluttered living room. A few minutes later, I'm curled up on his leather sofa, tossing back straight shots of Patrone.

"Feel better?" he asks.

The smile I give him feels heavy. "You know me. I take a lickin' and keep on tickin'."

"That's not funny."

"It wasn't meant to be." I pour another shot and toss it back.

"He loves you," Shakespeare says.

"Is that supposed to make it all better?"

"No." He takes the glass from my hand and pours himself a shot and then quickly another. "Truth is, I don't know what to tell you. A part of me wants you to leave him . . . and another part tells me if you do, it will destroy him."

"I can't save him," I say, feeling new tears brim my eyes. "I've tried."

He nods, pours another drink, and hands it to me.

Wordlessly I take it, and after I drain the glass I welcome the alcohol's fuzzy warmth like an old familiar lover. "I'm gonna leave him, you know." I don't look at him this time. "After I get my license and stuff. I have to."

"Where will you go?"

I can only shake my head; after all, I'm making

these plans up as I say them. "I want to be like you," I whisper. "I want to make something of myself. I want to be someone my children will be proud of. Someone they will admire."

"They are proud of you," he whispers back.

My face burns from the praise.

"It wasn't easy doing what you did. Four years clean, that's plenty to be proud of."

I shrug. "Maybe."

Shakespeare's hand lands on top of my knee. "I admire you."

My gaze shoots up to his sparkling eyes and that warm, fuzzy feeling becomes something hot and dangerous. It's all the warning I have before our lips find each other. The taste of his kiss is more potent than the Patrone and sweeter than anything I've ever known. Swear to God, all I could do is sigh and melt against him. But then Shakespeare comes to his senses and jumps to his feet and nearly trips over the coffee table.

"I'm sorry. I'm sorry. I don't know what got into me."

"Don't," I say, shaking my head and finding his gaze. "I'm not sorry at all." I stand up. "In fact, I've been waitin' for you to kiss me like that for a long time."

His eyes grow wide as he continues to shake his head. "You're my brother's wife."

I stalk toward him. "Your brother is not here."

"We can't," he says, but the protest sounds weak.

I take his hand and place it against my breast, willing him to feel my heartbeat. "Do you know how long it's been since I've felt like a woman? Do you know what it's like to ache deep in your soul for a soft touch or a light kiss? For someone to fill you up and awaken your senses?" I press his hand tighter against my chest. "You can do this for me. You can bring me back to life." I stare into his eyes and I can see him wavering.

"Keesh—"

"Shh." I press my finger against his lips. "Don't make me beg."

Our eyes lock and we stare at each other for a long time. Just when I think he's gonna turn me away, his head descends and our lips meet, our clothes disappear, and our naked skin kiss.

11

Princess

That Thursday after school, me and Lucky is sittin' in the hall outside their apartment. Usually Lucky loves talkin' 'bout boys, clothes, music videos, and stuff. But today is my turn to be as good a friend as she always is for me. It's my turn to listen to her troubles.

She pulls her legs to her chest and drops her head on her knees. My heart breaks as her shoulders shake with her tears. I ain't used to no emotions and stuff, so I just pick at a loose string on my jeans. But I can feel her hurt. I feel it like a motherfucker.

"It'll be okay, Lucky. Fuck him. He ain't good enough for you anyway," I say.

She lifts her head and looks at me. Her eyes are red and puffy. Snot and tears run down her face. She looks like hell. "I can't believe that fool fronted on me in front of that bitch like that. He fuckin' nasty-ass, crabby-ass, stank-ass Felisha right up in the bathroom at school. Everybody laughin' at me and shit. And he know I hate that bitch. I'm a beat her ass. You *know* I'm a beat her ass?"

Yup, I know she will. Lucky has all that strength and fight that been beat down out of me.

"And I had his dick in my mouth," she spat before she really did spit like she gettin' the taste of him off her tongue.

I could tell her that shit don't work. If it's as easy as spitting to get the memory of somebody's dick out your mouth, I woulda got over all that shit done to me a long time ago.

Lucky lets her head fall back against the graffiti-covered wall. "I love that nigga, Princess. I love him," she says soft as hell as she turns her head to the left to look down the hall out the window.

I sit closer to her and take her hand to squeeze because that's what she always does when I tell her about what all my momma's men done to me over the years. Sometimes just holding Lucky's hand keeps me from doing something crazy.

She squeezes my hand back before she reaches in her bookbag for her secret stash of cigarettes. She sees my eyes shoot to her front door. "My daddy 'sleep. He got to work the night shift."

She lights it and takes a long drag before she passes it to me to pull on. "Sing something for me?" she asks, sounding more like she's ten than seventeen.

I didn't really feel like singin' but if Lucky asks me to walk with her to South Carolina, I would do that shit for my girl for real.

"Shareefa?" I ask. We both like the singer so much 'cause her music reminds us of Mary J. *and* she's a homegirl living right here in the A-T-L.

"Yeah. Sing that slow version of her song "Cry No More" that you made up."

I close my eyes and tilt my head back as the words flow from me. I sing for her from my soul. That part of me that hold all them damn secrets and pain and shame. I have to admit that my voice sounds real good in the hall. Something called acoustics or some shit.

The door down at the end of the hall leading into the stairwell opens and this tall guy with a big-ass 'fro looks down the hall at us. He steps into the hall in a tight-ass camel leather motorcycle jacket, wifebeater, and oversized dark jeans with two big shopping bags in each hand. Diamonds or cubic zirconia, platinum, or silver—shit I ain't know the difference, but his jewelry is shining like crazy.

The rest of my words fade away as I drop my eyes from his. Lucky sticks her cigarette between her lips as she hurries to use her hands to wipe the tears and snot from her face.

"Which one of y'all shorties was just singing?" he asks, his grilles making his words sound heavy. He drops his bags to put his hands on the back of his oversized jeans to hitch them up while he walks down the hall toward us.

Lucky cuts her puffy eyes at me as she stands to her feet looking real cute in a pink Baby Phat jean suit. "That was her," she says, pointing her hand at me before she takes a long pull of her cigarette.

"That shit was mad crazy," he says, standing beside me as he looks down at me.

I hate the way I want to flinch just because he's a man and he's near me.

He smiles at me and I'm damn near blinded by the bling. "You can sing your ass off, girl."

I turn my head and look down at his fresh pair of suede camel Air Force 1s. I just nod my head. I'm nervous as shit. I'm always nervous and afraid around men.

"Who you is?" Lucky asks with all her boldness and confidence as she drops the cig to the floor and squashes it with the toe of her kicks.

He crosses his arms over his chest while he sizes Lucky up from head to toe. "Everybody calls me Danger. I'm a music producer."

That makes me tilt my head back to look up at his face.

"Ooh, you looking for somebody to be in your videos?" Lucky asks as she turns and jiggles her big old ghetto booty in a thousand different directions before she pop, lock, and drop it.

"No," he says, shaking his head at her like she crazy and should know better than dancing nasty in front of a man she don't hardly know. He shifts them black-ass eyes on me and I have to make myself not look away.

Hi, I'm Princess, I want to say, but I can't get the words out of my head.

"Who you work wit?" Lucky asks, reaching out to touch his arm. "Bobby Valentino? Luda? The Ying-Yang Twins? Ciara? Who? Huh? Who?"

He runs his tongue over his grilles as he looks at her like she's working his nerves.

Leave him alone, Lucky, I think.

"I'm working with some new talent here in Atlanta," he says, all proud and shit.

"Oh," Lucky says, all disappointed and shit.

"Don't flex, 'cause I'm about to blow up and own

my record label one day. All types of good shit comin' my way, ya heard me?" he tells Lucky as he slides his thumbs into his front pockets.

Then why you hanging around Bentley Manor, Mr. Gonna Be a Big-Time Producer?

"Shee-it, then why you hanging around *this* motherfucker?" Lucky asks.

I smile 'cause she says what I'm thinking . . . in her own way.

"You know what," he says suddenly as he points at Lucky. "You talk too much and your friend don't talk enough."

"She don't talk much," Lucky tells him, straight on my defense.

He squats down beside me and my heart damn near jumps up in my throat. Why can't I be normal, shit?

"There's a big-time talent contest at this community center downtown next Wednesday. You should enter. Your ass can blow them other chicks straight off the stage."

Danger reaches in his back pocket for one of them glossy flyers like they use to promote for club parties and car shows. He hands it to me.

I look at it and then back up at him before I take it. A talent contest? Singing in these pissy halls or in my room or in front of Lucky is different than getting up on somebody's stage. Shit, I don't even have the clit to do that shit. Not even.

"Look, I got to get this shit to my baby momma and get to the studio—"

His baby momma?

"Who your baby momma?" Lucky asks before she drops back down on the floor next to me.

He stands and walks away from us to snatch up his shopping bags. Dangerous-ass Danger laughs while he shakes his head. "Your young ass nosy as hell," he says before he turns and walks back down the hall.

"Inquiring minds want to know," she calls down to him.

He just laughs again before he pushes through the door to the stairwell.

I'm surprised that it's me that jumps to my feet with that flyer clutched in my hand. I go into the stairwell just to see him go through the door for the second floor.

"Big Princess," Lucky jokes as I walk back down the hall. "He *is* hella fine. Looking in his face made me forget Dean for a while," she says, suddenly sounding sad again.

I look down at the flyer and my eyes widen on the five-hundred-dollar first prize. "Lucky, you think I can really win this?" I ask, surprised that I am even giving any thought to this shit.

Lucky snatches up her bookbag and then jumps to her feet. She kicks the cigarette butt down the hall from the front of the apartment before she unlocks the door. "Not only do I think your ass can win it. You *gone* win it. Fuck that. It's your time."

It's my *time?*

The thought of that felt good. Damn good.

"How I look, Lucky?" I ask for the thousandth damn time as we stand backstage.

"You look like you 'bout to throw up," she jokes as she reaches over to give me a hug.

I try to laugh with her but I do feel sick as hell. But I have to do this. I want to do it. I *can* do it.

I'm going to sing my slow version of "Cry No More." All week long Lucky made me practice and practice. On the bus ride to school. In the bathroom at school during lunch. After school in the stairwell or in her room.

She asked her daddy for money for a new outfit and then spent the money on me 'cause she knew my momma wasn't shit. Hell, I didn't even tell her about the contest 'cause I didn't doubt my momma would enter and try to beat me to the first prize. Straight tri-flin'.

I still can't believe how good I look in these dark-denim skinny jeans and an off-the-shoulder white shirt. I have on a bunch of fake gold jewelry that will probably turn before I even get offstage. Keisha, Bentley Manor's own bootleg hairstylist, curled my hair and then pulled it all up into a side ponytail. Lucky did my makeup.

I look like me only better. Older. Prettier.

"BOO! BOO! WHOMP-WHOMP! WHOMP-WHOMP!"

Me and Lucky look at each other as the crowd goes Apollo Amateur Hour on somebody. The singing stops and the booing gets louder and louder.

"Fuck all y'all!" a guy screams in a high-pitched voice.

We jump out the way as a thin light-skinned dude with a jheri curl—or good-ass hair—comes running past us off the stage. Some of his activator must have hit the floor 'cause his ass goes sliding face-first into a wall.

What the fuck?

Everybody backstage is dying laughing. Everybody except Lucky and me. My ass is up next and karma is a bitch.

We hold hands as we walk closer to the curtain. "You can do this, Princess. You know I wouldn't lie to you. For real. You can do this."

The ruckus from the crowd quiets down and I hear my name being called.

Lucky holds my shaking body close and whispers in my ear, "If you get scared or nervous and all that shit just close your eyes and pretend you're in your bedroom window. I'm right here and if dem niggas out there flex then we'll just whup *all* they ass. Fuck it."

I hug her back real tight. Real real tight.

When the announcer calls my name again, I know I have to do this. Lucky steps back. I peek out and see all the people waiting to boo my ass off that damn stage. I close my eyes and start singing right there behind the curtain. The audience and the people backstage clap for me, and I feel Lucky's hand press to my back to push me out onstage.

I can't explain what comes over me. Shit, I don't know if it's them lights shining on me on that stage, or the people clapping and urging me on, or knowing Lucky is right there waiting to whup these motherfuckers' ass for me, or just my love of music, but when my ass hit that stage and *sang*, I ain't feel like quiet, nervous, sad, and sorrowful Princess. I ain't feel like me no more.

I open my eyes and sing into that mic as I remember to work the stage the way Lucky showed me. And I *work* that motherfucker. I stroll up and down that stage like it really is my time for *something* good to happen for me.

I stand in the middle of the stage giving myself goosebumps as I fling my head back and damn near taste the mic on my tongue as I hit a high note that is filled all up with the joy and happiness I feel . . . *for me.*

When I take my bow most of the audience is on their feet. As good as I feel, I have to force myself not to cry. I feel like I *do* have a voice. I *do* have something to say. Somebody wants to listen to me.

I hand the announcer the mic and run into Lucky's arms. As we jump up and down, I wonder if my momma knew what I just accomplished if her ass would even be proud of me.

That night as I lay on my twin bed in the darkness I can't even sleep. I'm too excited. I pull my diary from underneath my pillow and go to sit in the windowsill. The light from the streetlamp is just enough for me to see as I write:

> *I won! I won! I won! I still can't believe it and*
> *I have nobody but Lucky to thank for it. She*

was surprised when I gave her half the prize money but she deserves that and more. She's the only good person left in my life and I would have given her all of it if she woulda took it. She was just as excited as me when Danger came over to me and gave me a piece of paper with the address to this studio. He wants me to sing background or something on one of those "up and comers" he working with. Me on somebody's record? Danger said I could blow up and be as big as Keyshia Cole or even THE Mary J. Blige. Me. He said he would pay me a little something, too. Regardless of where this singing thing takes me and that's hopefully up outta Bentley Manor, Lucky is going with me. Together me and my friend can do anything. It's OUR time.

12

Takiah

"C'mon. Just one hit. I'll suck your cock. I'll do anything you want. Just give me one hit and I swear I'll pay you back."

Hassan's striking green eyes fill with disgust as he looks at me, and I really don't give a shit.

"Takiah, there ain't shit you can do for me but go home and take care of your baby."

Guilt crashes through me at the reminder that I left Tanana sleeping in the middle of my bed while Grandma Cleo left to take Miz Osceola to her podiatrist appointment. It also means that I have a limited amount of time to score this hit. Shit, I've been back in Bentley Manor for seven weeks and I really need a hit bad.

"C'mon, Hassan. Help a sistah out. I promise I'll

make you feel real good." I reach for the front of his pants and this motherfucker grabs my hands so hard, I swear he's trying to snap them off.

"Get your goddamn hands off of me!" He pushes me away and I feel my chances of scoring fading. "Give me twenty-four hours; I swear I'll get the money for you."

He only laughs. "My name ain't Visa. I don't run shit off credit."

"Please," I beg, feeling my tears swell.

"Go home, Takiah."

I stare after him as he turns his back and walks away from me. It's all I can do not to drop to my knees and start sobbing like a thrown-away child. When I hang my head, my eyes fall to the band around my finger.

"Hassan," I shout, running toward him and pulling at the gold band around my finger. "Here." I stuff the ring into his hand. "It's real gold."

He looks disappointed in me, but in the end hands over three vials of crack to complete our business transaction.

When I return to Grandma Cleo's apartment, I'm relieved to see Tanana is still sleeping in the center of my twin-sized bed. I find my tattered duffel bag at the bottom of the bedroom's closet and pull out my beloved glass pipe. I'm practically salivating and barely able to keep my hand steady as I go through the motions. On my first puff, tears fill my eyes and I swear this shit is like one big-ass orgasm, causing my tits to harden and my legs to shake.

Ah, this is the shit.

This takes me away from the world and its problems. Since I hadn't been a Georgia resident in a while, it's taking longer to get government help for my baby, and Grandma Cleo keeps talkin' 'bout me gettin' a job.

Shit. I don't know how to do nothin'. And I damn sure ain't about to go get some minimum-wage job asking folks if they want fries with their burgers. You got me twisted.

What I need is a man, boyfriend, or sugar daddy that's gonna take care of me and Tanana. Despite the way Hassan had looked at me, there are plenty of men who would still love to get with this. Trust.

I'm only good at stealin' and fuckin' and that's the honest-to-God truth. Nobody knows how fucked up that is more than I do. Now that that ex junkie, Keisha, is going to school, it's all Grandma Cleo talks about.

"Why can't you be more like her? If Keisha can clean up her act anybody can," Miz Nosceola always cosigns.

Fuck Keisha.

If Keisha was such a saint, how come her man is out here selling her damn kids' toys, tryna get high or whupping her ass like it ain't shit all the time?

Keisha is just as fucked up as I am and the bitch knows it.

The phone rings and I nearly jump out my skin thinkin' it's my grandma chargin' through with the cavalry. Trust when I say she will stone-cold whup my ass if she caught me smokin' this shit in her house. I draw in another deep puff thinkin' this high would be worth whateva trouble down the road.

I slump over the floor, completely ignoring the ringing phone. Another puff and I swear I can feel the soft mush of my brain floating inside my head. That shit always trips me out. Lowering the pipe to the floor, I'm vaguely aware that I need to put the shit up, but I'm too fascinated about how good everything feels right now: my face, my chest, my breasts. I give them a little squeeze and pinch and another orgasm shoots off through my quivering clit.

Ah. Thank you, Jesus. I needed this shit so bad.

Yes, I know I should be ashamed for thanking Him for this hit, but you just don't know how good this shit makes me feel. It feels good to stop the worrying.

I curl onto the floor, enjoying my high. Vaguely, I'm aware of the other two vials of rock on the floor. No need to waste those motherfuckers, 'cause I won't get another chance like this to be alone once Grandma Cleo comes home.

I quickly load up the pipe again, determined to get higher than I've been in a while.

And I succeed.

I just wish I'd gotten that last vial of crack off the floor before I fell asleep and my baby woke up.

13

Woo Woo

"Are you happy?" Lexi asks me as we walk into the parking deck of Phipps Plaza.

I slip my new Fendi shades on and laugh. "Hell, yeah. Why?" I ask, even though I know my words are a damn lie. I've been married for almost two months and I'm not any closer to getting Hassan up outta my system.

"Just doing my job as a sister and checking on you." She throws me a half smile that says more than her words.

She's worried about me.

"What about you? It's been a minute since we talked about Luth—"

Lexi's eyes flash with anger and way more hatred than anybody should have illuminating from their eyes. "Don't you dare mention that motherfucker's name to me. Fuck him."

Walking in on your husband in the shower with one of your baby daddies *will* put all that anger in a woman's soul.

"Shit, I feel you on that. *Fuck* him."

I change the subject. That shit with Luther and Junior really touches her hard. Now she don't even fuck with any dudes, and I can't ever remember my sister being without a man . . . ever. That chick don't do shit but go to work and hang out with her kids. Considering her track record with men, maybe that's a good damn thing.

We go our separate ways when we got to our cars. I sit in my Honda lighting a cigarette while Lexi pulls off in her old Lincoln, Black Betty, with a honk of her horn. I put in my Young Buck CD and turn up the volume until the bass feels like it's booming inside my chest. I start dancing right in my seat before I roll down the window, light a Black & Mild, and pull out of the parking spot. I'm just turning onto the first level of the parking deck when I see Hassan about to unlock the door of his gold 2000 Lexus SC400.

How could I forget how much he shops. That motherfucker went to the mall like twice a week just spending up that fast dope money. Same way he used to spend it on me. Some of the best gear I own came from Hassan.

I force myself to drive the hell on by and he happens to look up over his shoulder and see me. That crazy motherfucker steps right into the path of my car, and there ain't shit I can do but slam on my brakes. Shit, this pussy really got Hassan going crazy.

Damn. He looking good as hell. Real good.

I am *loving* the colorful navy blue, red, and yellow print Roca Wear hood he wore with faded jeans and matching colorful Air Force 1s. His shoulder-length sandy hair is braided in a crazy design. His jewelry is iced the fuck out and I'm turned the fuck on.

Damn. Damn. Damn. My hands start to sweat as Hassan comes around to my driver's-side window. I turn the music down.

"Whaddup, WooWoo," he says in that husky voice. He holds a lit blunt between his soft kissable lips as he looks down at me with them sexy-ass green eyes. "Long time no see."

I reach up with more boldness than I feel and take the blunt from his mouth. After two long drags I release the thick haze of smoke through my nose as I watch Hassan through squinted eyes. "Just been livin' life, you know."

"That Oreo motherfucker done changed you and

shit." Hassan reaches out to take the blunt back from me. "What, you some suburbia chick or some shit now? Fuck the hood? Fuck this hood nigga?"

My pussy lips clap as he deliberately licks the tip like he trying to taste me.

He bends down to lean inside the window and the scent of his Black Polo cologne fills my car. My lungs. My soul. I take a deep breath of it. Damn. Damn. Diggety damn damn.

"That's some fucked-up shit, coming to my crib to fuck me and getting your ass right up that morning to marry that other fool. The *next* fucking morning. That's some real ill shit, WooWoo. Ain't tell a mother-fucker nothing. I got to hear in the street your ass got married. What the fuck is up with you? It's like you said fuck me like that fucking Oreo nigga is better than me or some shit."

I have to admit that the anger in his eyes is a little scary. He ain't ever flipped on me, but I done seen him wild-out before, and I want no parts of that shit.

He stands up suddenly and swaggers over toward his car as he wipes his mouth and swaggers back. "Don't be scared of me," he says, bending back down to kiss my cheek. "You know I wouldn't do shit to hurt you."

"I don't think you would hurt me intentionally, but you let your anger fuck with you until your ass can't see straight and that's not good. I mean you really gone hurt somebody or get yourself hurt just raging out like that."

Hassan drops his eyes from mine.

"Hell, I heard you and old lady Cleo got into it. Said you cussed her out and threatened her or some shit?"

"That old bitch gone ask me if I sold her crack-head granddaughter dope . . . like I'm gone cop to anything to her ass and she ain't shit but the police." Hassan's mouth twisted. "Blaming me for her ass gettin' high and that nasty bitch gone beg me to sell to her. Talkin' 'bout she'll suck my cock. My *cock*? Where the hell she from any fucking way?"

There is no denying the anger blazing in his eyes. "Talkin' that bullshit 'bout turning me in to the police or some shit. She gone turn in her crackhead granddaughter too for using dope? Hell, naw, I'm the only bad one. Man, fuck that shit and fuck that old bitch, man."

"Hassan, that's an old lady!"

He shoves his hands into the front pockets of his jeans, but I can tell from the imprint that he opening and closing his hands into fists. "Nobody fucks with me, my money, or my freedom. Fuck that. I'm serious as a heart attack about this shit, yo."

And I did know that.

"That's one of the reasons we couldn't make it. 'Cause straight up? I don't know if you gone flip on me like that and I wake up with a gun in my mouth like a fucking dick."

Hassan scrunched up his face as he looked down at me before he smiles. "WooWoo, your ass is crazy," he says before he smokes his blunt like it's a Newport. "A gun ain't shit like a dick. It's a lot more poppin' off than a damn nut."

"Shut up, boy."

"Boy?"

"Whateva." I wave my hand.

Hassan bends down and moves in close to me. As his lips move down to my neck, my head falls back against the headrest. I ain't ever had somebody who can make me wet and hot that damn fast. I try to think of my husband as Hassan sticks his hands down between my legs to massage my pussy through the leggings I wore with a tight-fitting sweater and belt— all BCBG. Damn, I try and try to think about Reggie like a motherfucker, but before I know it that sexy bitch is opening my door and turning me around to push down across the front seats.

I ain't give a shit 'bout nothin' as Hassan jerks them leggings down over my hips. Not my husband. Not the gear shift pressing into my back. Not the fact that we in the middle of the exit lane in the parking deck. Not the cool October air blowing against my bare ass. Nothing. Fuck it. Shit.

He pushes my wet-ass thong to the side and drops to his knees right there on the damn ground. I shiver as he lowers his head to blow cool air against my pussy before he licks away. I bend my legs to really let him get at it and one of my knees hit the horn but he ain't stopping sucking on my clit one damn bit.

"Make that bitch cum, Has," I moan as I circle my hips up against his mouth.

Like a soldier that bitch takes directions good as hell and sucks deeper on my clit until I'm holding the back of his braided head as I jerk my hips up against his mouth. My knee keeps hitting the horn as I holler out roughly. My cum fills his mouth and my clit tingles like crazy. No one or nothing is better.

Someone lays on their horn and we both jerk our heads up to look out the back window at a line of cars held up behind me. He laughs as he kisses both my thighs and then rises to his feet. "Next time your man fucking you think about that shit," he tells me before he leaves my exposed ass right there to climb into his car. The bass of his system makes the change rattle in my car as he reverses his car and then pulls away out the deck.

The people lay on their horns again. "Shut the fuck up," I scream out the window as I try to stop my legs and shit from shaking. I sit up, pressing my wet ass to my leather seat as I lean down and snatch my leggings from the cement before I swing my legs in and close my door.

"Nasty ass," somebody screams out the window of one of the cars behind me.

I flip them the bird and speed out of the parking deck. I got to get home and wash before Reggie gets there. Since he only works half a day on Saturdays, my ass is going to test the speed limits. I hope the cops don't pull me over. How the hell can I explain riding through A-T-L in nothing but a cum-filled thong?

I knew I had a choice to make. My fate was in my own hands. I made my choice: Reggie, marriage, life in the 'burbs, my new look, my new life. It was all my decision. It was all my own choice.

Hassan can't offer me the things Reggie can and will. Hassan will never marry me. He will never leave the hood. That nigga? Shit, he's a ghetto baby for life. He probably never dreams outside the borders of the hood. He probably ain't know shit but slinging drugs, and everybody know that shit is a one-way street. Once you start down that motherfucking road and get hooked on the life—the same way the customers get hooked on that shit—there is no turning back. And there's nothing at the end of that road but death or jail.

What woman—what grown-ass woman—would choose that kind of life, not knowing if your man gone make it alive on the streets in the daytime, get busted on the block at night, or drag you under with him tomorrow?

With Reggie I didn't have to worry about 5-0 busting in my house looking for dope and money. When he leaves in the morning to go to work, I pray for his safe return, but I don't have to pray that he doesn't get shot by some up-and-coming, go-getter motherfuckers who want to get rid of their street competition. I don't have to pray that he forever and ever outruns the police.

Fucking around with Hassan, I know a dozen ways for a head to smoke crack. You'd be amazed what them motherfuckers can do with an empty soda can, a stick pin, and some fucking ashes.

Dealing with Reggie, I know a dozen ways to save money. Shit, who knew that a CD meant more than an artist's latest release? My ass sure didn't.

The life I woulda had with Hassan and the life I have with Reggie are two entirely different things.

It's true Reggie ain't know shit about the hood except what he hears on TV or reads in the papers. He don't have a clue about hood struggle. Single mother with five kids in a two-bedroom trailer having to sell food stamps for cash just to pay her bills. Living in a shit hole like Bentley Manor 'cause you couldn't afford higher rent 'cause your ass dropped out of a school system that is lacking like a motherfucker any damn way. Having to shop at grocery stores and corner stores that smell like rotten meat 'cause the owners know your ass is gone shop there anyway—and then they overcharge you for the right to shop in their stank-ass stores. Ain't *that* a bitch? Kids having to drop to the ground at the sound of gunshots like they in Iraq or some shit. Sistahs working hard at fast-food restaurants and as maids at hotels and cashiers at gas stations just to bring home two hundred dollars every two weeks.

That's the kind of shit Reggie doesn't understand and probably doesn't give a fuck about either. That's the shit, the life, Hassan and I have in common.

But I don't hold that against Reggie. He couldn't no more control being born in the burbs than I could control my crackhead momma having me in the hood. I don't blame him and shit. But sometimes I feel like he blames me. He's never really said shit about it, but any monkey can see we're different and he has to think his way is the better way—the only way.

I don't want to lose my husband. I don't want to lose my life. I don't want to cheat on my husband.

But . . .

Here I am again.

I park Black Betty, my sister's '91 Continental, on the side of the Circle K down the block from Bentley Manor. There's a few fellas lounging against the building, but I don't recognize any of them, so I go inside the convenience store and buy five peach Phillies blunts and a forty-ounce of Old English—Hassan's version of fine champagne. As I leave the building I reach for my cell phone and dial Lexi's house.

"Hey. Did Reggie call back?"

I hear her yawn. "Not since the last time he called and spoke to you an hour ago."

"Good." I walk up the broken concrete sidewalk toward Bentley Manor. "You left my car outside your garage, right?"

"Yes. Yes. Yes. Now where your trickin' ass at anyway?" she asks.

I can't tell my sister I'm dealing with Hassan. No way in *hell* I can tell her that. Shit, I don't want anybody to know about us. That's why my ass is sneaking around at one in the morning like a fiend. Shit. I'm a junkie a'ight. I'm gonna get me a Hassan fix.

"Stop being so nosy," I tell her as I turn the corner around the front gate.

"And you stop using me for an alibi and lying on my kids' health to go fuck around on your husband."

Bentley Manor's parking lot is empty—that's rare—but I throw my hoodie up around my head anyway as I make my way to Hassan's building.

"I gotta go. I'll call you when I'm on the way back."

"Woo Woo—"

I close my phone and turn it off as I jog up the stairs and knock on his door. I look up and down the hall as I wait for him. I didn't call first 'cause I didn't want him to tell me not to come. But I know he's home. His car is parked in its usual spot downstairs.

I touch the door like it will make me feel closer to him.

"Who?"

I knock lightly three times. It's our signal. The door opens and I feel like I am let into heaven.

As soon as I step inside, I reach for him, but he steps back from me. "Why you here, WooWoo?" he asks.

I look him dead in them eyes and speak from my heart. "Because I'm in love with you and I can't live without you in my life. I can't do it. I tried. I really tried but I can't. I love you. I love you *so* much."

Hassan pulls me into his arms and *now* I feel like I'm really home.

14

Keisha

I don't want to go home.

For the second time in three weeks, Smokey has tried to kill me. This time the snooty brunette with the paramedics talked me into going to the emergency room. Prognosis: a concussion and one broken rib.

I'll live.

The kids couldn't stay with Miz Cleo. I had to drop them off at my not-too-happy sister's, since Cleo was in the middle of handling her own emergency with Takiah and the baby.

Shit always happens in threes, but around here shit just happens all the time.

Miz Osceola squawked to all who would listen that she and Miz Cleo had arrived home just in time to stop Tanana from ingesting some drugs, while her momma slept high as a kite on the floor. My heart lurched because that is an everyday fear with my own children.

Miz Osceola stood, proud as she pleased on her cemented porch, waving her Lousiville Slugger at a few of Kaseem's foot soldiers and promising if she ever found out who sold Takiah those drugs, she was going to show them how things were done back in the ol' Negro Baseball League.

No one doubted that she would.

And no one talked.

In a way, it's funny. All these tough, hard-core thugs runnin' around here, and they're all scared to cross two old ladies with baseball bats. Hell, I'd buy a bat myself, but I know the moment I turned around or left the house that son of a bitch would be down at the pawn shop.

Smokey is nothing if not predictable.

"I'm gonna clean up," my husband says from the backseat of Shakespeare's Dodge Intrepid.

The car is deathly silent after this announcement.

"I mean it this time," he emphasizes, almost pleading for belief.

I cut a glance over to Shakespeare behind the driver's seat. The instant poundin' in my heart ushers in a tidal wave of guilt. The fact that he won't return my gaze speaks volumes.

Things have changed.

My gaze shifts back to the car-clogged expressway and then down to study the floor mat.

"Keisha?" Smokey's rough and ashy hand plops down onto my shoulder. I close my eyes as he gives it an affectionate squeeze and tears that I long thought had dried resurfaced.

"I'm sorry, baby," he sobs and sniffs. "You know I don't mean to hurt you . . . don't you?"

But you always do.

"I'm going to rehab."

Again?

"I don't really want you to give up your schoolin'. I want you to do what makes you happy," he says, tryin' his best to sound like a Hallmark card. "I'm gonna clean up. You'll see."

Same shit, different day.

Holloway Parkway comes into view. My stomach twists into multiple knots at the sight of Bentley Manor's tall, wrought-iron gate. Clusters of different groups of people are spread throughout.

On one end there are young teenage girls with bodies older than their minds while, at the other, teenage boys in cheap jewelry and clothes three sizes too big gawk and make lewd comments. In between: rude children, Kaseem's foot soldiers, and shakin' junkies. Home sweet home.

Damn.

Shakespeare parks the car, but it's a few, long, agonizin' seconds before he shuts off the motor. I don't blame him. He's just as tired of this routine as I am.

Still, I wish the uneasiness between us would disappear. We did it. It was a mistake. It will never happen again.

I swallow hard.

How many times have I told myself this in the past three weeks? When will it start to *feel* like it was a mistake? And how come it can't happen again?

Damn, I'd forgotten how to be a woman until that night at Shakespeare's house. I'd forgotten what it felt like to be wanted and desired. And for every second of the last three weeks, all I can think about is how much I loved the way Shakespeare's mouth, hands, and long, smooth dick drove me to ecstasy.

How can I keep calling something like that a mistake?

Why can't we do it again and again?

Smokey opens the back car door. I also scramble out and follow him to our apartment building with my head hung low.

With it being the weekend and everyone hangin' out, I don't doubt there are a few fingers pointing and gums bumpin' about our business. What else is there to do around here?

Our sofa of the month is a tan-and-cream–checkered number that's older than I am. I picked it out at the Salvation Army. I'd done my best to clean it up, but to be honest only God can perform the kind of miracle it needs. For now it'll have to do.

Shakespeare brought up the rear and closed the door behind him after entering the apartment.

"Yo, bro," Smokey says, embracing him. "Thanks again. And I mean what I said in the car. I gonna get my act together."

Shakespeare's thick braids bob as he tries to return his brother's smile.

Has it finally happened? Has he finally given up hope on Smokey gettin' clean? Believe it or not, I never thought this day would come. I always thought if I ever gave up the fight for my husband's sobriety that I could always count on Shakespeare to hang in there.

"I think I'm goin' to start with a good hot shower," Smokey declares, tryin' his best to remain upbeat. Did he sense he'd finally pushed us too far?

Maybe.

I just know I have a hard time meetin' his gaze, scared that he will see my doubt, exhaustion, and guilt.

Smokey turns toward me, beamin' his still remarkably white teeth and jerking me into a fierce hug. "I love you, baby."

The hug is too tight, and despite my mental urging, I can't make myself hug him back. When he pulls away, he hunts down and traps my troubled gaze. "Don't give up on me," he pleads, his voice sounding like broken glass.

Those goddamn tears return and I hear myself lying, "I won't."

Satisfied, Smokey delivers an almost fatherly peck to my forehead. "That's my girl." He turns and gives his brother a mock salute. "Later, bro."

"Later."

Smokey whistles his way toward the bathroom like he doesn't have a care in the world. Who knows. Maybe he doesn't.

Shakespeare and I make a great show of bouncing our gazes around the room until we hear the shower come on and Smokey's off-key singing fills the apartment.

"I better go." Shakespeare turns for the door.

"Wait." I don't know what I want to say beyond

that, but my heart leaps when he stops with his hand frozen on the doorknob.

"It was a mistake, Keesh," he whispers, as if Smokey may hear him over the shower.

"I don't love him."

He rolls his head and stares up at the ceiling. "He's my brother."

"And he's my husband."

With a sigh, his hands fall away from the doorknob and he turns and faces me. "Those are two good reasons why—"

"I love you."

His face stretches in agony. "C'mon, Keesh. Don't make this harder than it already is."

"How can it possibly get any harder than this?" I ask, approaching. I no longer recognize my voice and I feel like I'm choking on my words. "What happened a few weeks ago—"

"Keesh—"

"Changed my life," I continue, not wanting him to interrupt. "I've been dead inside for so long. I've been living this fucked life somehow thinking that I deserve it. But guess what, I don't deserve it." I lay a hand against his arm, his muscles flex beneath my fingertips. "I deserve you."

The look he gives me scares me for a moment. It's

a look that tells me he doesn't feel the same way I do. The woman he spent a lifetime loving died in his arms months ago at the gates of this hellhole. For him, what happened between us three weeks ago had nothing to do with love and everything to do about filling a void: loneliness.

Fuck. I'll take what I can get.

I take his arms and direct them around my waist. "It's okay. You don't have to love me back." I ease up onto my toes and press a kiss against his full lips.

Fresh tears blur my vision when he doesn't kiss me back. I'm a little more insistent on my second kiss, when I slip my tongue between his plump lips and slide it against his silky tongue.

Goddamn, it feels like heaven.

Smokey's singing continues to fill the house as I pull Shakespeare's shirt over his head and then attack the buttons of his pants.

"We shouldn't be doing this," he says, finally kissing me back.

He may not love me, but I still have what he needs. I plan on giving it to him until we're both satisfied, or at least until my husband gets out of the shower.

15

Princess

"You got it, Princess. Come on out."

I smile at Danger through the glass as I take off the headphones in the recording booth. When he smiles at me, I smile right on back, and my heart skips a beat as I leave the booth. The smell of weed and cognac is thick as hell as Danger and his boys combine partying with working in the studio.

Lucky is there waiting to throw her arm around my neck to hug me close. "Girl, you sounded so good. That's my dawg," she says, doing the two-step as she winks at me all playful and shit.

She moves to sit on the lap of Man, Danger's twenty-year-old brother, who looks as fine as Chance from *I Love New York*. I sit down on one of the cracked stools on either side of Danger as he plays the track back.

The song reminds me of Method Man and Mary's "You're All I Need." I look over at Q to see if he likes our work. His dreads swing back and forth a little as he bobs his head to Danger's track. He's mouthing his lyrics and motioning with his hands like he's in the club partying to his favorite song.

It's kinda crazy hearing myself, my voice, come through the speakers loud as hell.

"That's you, baby," Danger screams over my vocals. He holds out one of his thin hairy arms and pushes up the sleeves of his Coogi long-sleeved graphic tee. "Fucking goose bumps!"

I don't even realize I'm smiling until the track fades away.

Danger stands and hitches his pants up. "Princess, your ass is the truth. Your voice is on some real ill shit," he says with his grilles shining like the sun.

My heart skips another beat. I can't believe that for the first time ever I have a crush on a boy—well, a grown man. What's weird is Danger treats me like nothing but a little sister. Maybe it's my age or my mostly no-name clothes and homemade hairdos or my shyness. All I know is I want him to look at me different.

"Thanks," I say, still all shy and shit.

He throws his arm around my shoulder and my nipples get real hard. I have to cross my arms over my chest to keep anybody from seeing them poke through my faded, old-ass Baby Phat shirt. "Princess, let me holla at you for a second," he tells me before he leads me toward the door.

"Lucky, I'll be right back," I tell her over my shoulder.

"No problem," she says as she crosses her legs and pokes out her chest. She toots her lips for Man's blunt. Just like her little slave or some shit, he leans over to stick that motherfucker right in her mouth as his other hand moves up her leg to smack her ass.

Lucky is way over Dean and Funky Felisha. Way, way over. Hearing that scandalous chick is pregnant helped her through it. Shit, it helped Felisha out that ass-whippin' Lucky been plottin' to put on that bitch for real. This time Felisha is the lucky one because my friend draws the line at fucking up pregnant bitches. Lucky love da kids.

As Danger pushes open the door of the small studio—which really ain't shit but a converted storefront—I have to squint my eyes to get used to the late afternoon sun.

The cold whips at my ass and I wish like hell that I grabbed my jacket. It's nippy as a bitch out there.

"Listen, I was thinking maybe once we get Q's shit sold to a label and I get my production company better situated, I'd like to work with you on your own demo, Shorty."

Say what? Say fucking who? "For real?" I ask as I look up at him as the sun frames his freshly braided head.

Danger reaches in his back pocket for a soft pack of Newports. He pulls one out and lights it. "Hell, yeah. Your voice is the livest female shit I heard in a while."

I start to ask him for a cig but the last time I did he slapped me lightly on the nose and told me it's a bad habit. So I didn't fuck with it. "I can write music, too," I say, surprising myself that I'm able to speak up for my damn self.

He nods as he looks down at me. "I'm keepin' it funky with you right now. Paying for this studio time set a nigga back, so it might take a minute to get this shit going. But I promise you as soon as I get my set straight I want to work with you."

The door opens and Q walks out talking on his BlackBerry. He holds it up from his mouth. "I gotta roll, but call me," he says to Danger, not even looking at me before he gives him a pound and walks away up the busy downtown Atlanta street.

That ain't shit new. He's hardly said ten words to me during the two weeks we worked on his demo together. Most times that nigga act like I ain't around. Who cares?

Danger and I walk into the building past the makeshift receptionist area to the studio in the back. Another one of Danger's tracks is booming against the walls. Lucky's crazy ass is bent over in front of Man, booty dancing while he slaps at her ass with a white hand towel.

"Pop it, Man," she tells him in a singsong fashion while she jiggles that monster like a big old bowl of Jell-O.

"Shake it, Lucky," he answers with the blunt between his strong white teeth as he wrings the towel before he lets one end fly to hit her ass. *POP!*

"Pop it, Man."

"Shake it, Lucky."

"Pop it, Man."

"Shake it—"

"Y'all motherfuckers is stupid," Danger says before he starts gathering up his stuff to throw in a leather duffel bag.

I just laugh because Lucky *always* finds a way to have a good damn time. "Girl, you crazy."

The battered door to the small studio opens and I

smile right on through my disappointment to see Sade, Danger's girlfriend, stroll in. She frowns and makes a nasty face at Lucky, who keeps right on dancing with a suck of her teeth.

"Pop it, Man."

"Shake it, Lucky."

"Pop it, Man."

Sade, who isn't the same chick as his baby momma from up in Bentley Manor, just rolls her baby blue contacts before she wraps her arms around Danger and presses her curvaceous body against him as they kiss like they 'bout to fuck right there against the damn wall.

I look away because I wish I had her body. Her clothes. Her tight-ass blond weave. Her light-ass skin. Her jewelry. Her clothes. Her life. Her man.

"Come on, Lucky, we got to go." I walk over and pick up my bookbag.

"You go 'head. I'll take her home," Man says with his eyes on Lucky.

She shakes her head. "No, we gots shit to do but I'll get up with you another time," Lucky says, surprising the shit out of me.

"Bye y'all." I sneak one last glance at Danger smiling down in Sade's face.

"Hey, Man, this for the road," Lucky calls from the door as she makes her booty clap with a laugh and another eye roll at Sade.

"Them bitches need somebody to upgrade they broke-down ass," Sade said just as the door closes behind me. I didn't tell Lucky what I overheard because she woulda went right back in there and jacked that bitch up . . . before she fucked that bitch up.

We start walking up Peachtree, headed to the bus stop. "Damn, you turned Man down?" I ask.

"Fuck him. I ain't want shit but his weed. That nigga fine but I ain't lookin' for no damn dick. Shit. There's more to life than a sore wet ass."

We laugh as we walk and we don't even care that people look at us like we crazy.

"Guess what Danger said?"

"That he loves you just as much as you love him," she jokes as she bumps her shoulder against mine.

I mean-mug her ass and she starts laughing.

"Oops. I'm supposed to carry that you loving you some Danger to my grave, right?"

"Don't talk about it, be about it," I joke. I couldn't really get mad at Lucky.

There is commotion coming from behind us and we both turn to see two girls straight wilding out.

"It's a fight, Princess. Oh shit them bitches fighting." Lucky covers her open mouth with both her hands. *"Dayum!"*

Them chicks is swinging with their dukes up like two dudes. One of 'em shirt and bra is ripped in half and flappin' down around her waist. One of her big-ass titties is swingin' out free as ever like a third damn hand. The girl she is fighting is twice her size.

The girls come together biting and kicking and punching and the crowd around them is hollering like they ass is watching a real boxing match. When the girls come apart, they call each other everything *but* a child of God before they battle again. The crowd circles the girls, blocking them from our view.

"Oh shit, I can't see," Lucky says, turning to walk right toward the commotion.

"Come back, Lucky, I don't want to see no damn fight," I yell at her.

She turns to look at me over her shoulder and waves her hand for me to follow her before she disappears into the crowd.

I start walking down the street toward the fight. My mind is set on pulling Lucky's ass from that shit so we can catch the bus back to Bentley Manor. As I reach the outskirts of the circle, somebody hollers out loud as hell. It reminded me of something from a scary movie or some shit. It gives me chills.

"Oh shit. Oh shit, she stabbed her! She stabbed her!" The crowd starts running in a thousand different directions.

"Lucky," I call out. My eyes dart from left to right as I look for her face while people run past me.

An older guy is kneeling next to a body lying half in and half out the gutter. "What the—"

I run toward them. I try like hell to make myself believe that what I see isn't fucking true. I start shaking, and I gasp as I look down at my friend—my only friend—lying there with a knife stuck in her chest as her blood pools the street. I fall to the ground on my knees.

"One of them gals fighting stabbed her by mistake," the old man says as he rests his old wrinkled hand on my shoulder. "I called the police."

I shake him the fuck off as I bend down and pull her bloody body into my lap. My tears come fast and drip down my face to fall onto hers. "Don't you leave me, Lucky," I say through my snot and my tears.

"She gone. I'm sorry, but she already gone."

I don't need to hear his words. I knew as soon as I saw her that Lucky, *my* Lucky, is dead. I drop my head on top of hers and let out a scream that comes from deep down in my soul.

16

Takiah

"I almost killed my baby."

The horrible words tumble from my lips and spill onto my lap just like my tears of remorse. I try to remember all the details of that day, but I can't. The only things that remain in my mind are how badly I needed a hit and how wonderful that first puff felt hitting my bloodstream.

Fuck. I'm a junkie and I'm not sure I want to quit . . . not even for my little girl.

Life at Grandma Cleo's has yet to be the same. I'm no longer allowed to be home alone when Grandma has to run out for errands, and she throws one hell of fight to leave me alone with my own baby. Maybe I need to pack my shit and go somewhere else.

But where?

"How does that make you feel?" Pastor Meyer asks from behind his big expensive desk.

"How the fuck do you think it makes me feel?"

Pastor Meyer's eyebrows shoot up so fast, it's comical.

"Sorry," I say, but I'm not really. If you ask a stupid question then you should be prepared for anything. But this behavior isn't going to get me anywhere. The only way Grandma Cleo allows me to stay at her place now is because I agreed to have counseling sessions with Pastor Meyer.

Ain't I lucky?

"Tell me about your husband?" he asks.

I laugh for a while, and when I realize he's serious, I say, "Ain't much to tell."

"Where is he right now?"

"Where do you think he's at?"

"Jail?"

"Not bad. One guess and you got it right. Too bad I don't have a prize to give you."

"Is this how you hide your pain—behind a wall of sarcasm?"

"Is this how you make your money—stating the obvious?"

He actually laughs.

"Look, Takiah. I'm not trying to waste your time

and I'll appreciate it if you don't waste mine." His pointed gaze sears mine. I shift uncomfortably on his expensive leather couch. Jesus apparently pays pretty damn good.

"Look." I struggle for the right words. "Kameron is where he belongs."

"Why do you say that?"

"Because he fucked up my life," I shout, and then lower my voice. "Because he turned me into a junkie and a ho. I hope he rots there."

The silence in Pastor Meyer's office lasts so long I feel like we're playing some kind of game. When I can't stand it anymore, I continue. "Look, I'd done good. I lived eighteen years in Bentley Manor without ever developing a drug habit."

His eyebrows did their little seesaw thing, but I pretty much ignore them.

"Sure, I pulled a few childish pranks. Stole a few candy bars or what have you. But I made it out, goddammit, and now I'm right back where I started from." A sob tangles up on the last few words and I feel the threat of tears. "You don't know what it's like to take one step forward just to be dragged two steps back. Now I have to spend my life fightin' against somethin' I'm not strong enough to win."

"Have you talked to God?"

My laugh is immediate. "Give me a break. God doesn't even know my name."

"Don't be silly. Of course he does."

I slump back into the couch. "Then he has a funny way of showing it."

"He shows it every day," Pastor Meyer says with a wide smile. "Just think about all the people who didn't wake up this morning."

"Lucky bastards."

He releases another laugh. "I see if I don't watch you, you'll get me in a whole lot of trouble."

"Trouble is my middle name,'" I say, enjoying this unexpected camaraderie.

The silence returns while Pastor Meyer holds my gaze. There's something about his polished black eyes that gives me the sensation that he's dissecting me like a biology frog or something. Am I really worthy of the kingdom of heaven or is he just wasting his time?

If he's truly wondering, I can give him the answer. I'm lost and God isn't looking for me.

"You should give your life over to our Lord and Savior, Jesus Christ."

"I should do a lot of things," I say, shrugging, feeling a little disappointed in him. However, my statement is true. I *should* do a lot of things. I should be a better mom to my baby girl. I should try to get a job, even if it is dishing out fries. I should try to forget the horrible life I led in D.C with Kameron.

All these things are better said than done, and no matter what Grandma Cleo or the good pastor says, dropping to my knees and praying to some invisible god isn't going to make the pain go away. It's not going to erase my taste for crack.

Hell, I could use a hit now. Just a small one, something to just tie me over and let me sleep a little better tonight. Something that will quiet my periodic urges to inflict harm on myself, to my grandma, and even my little girl.

I mean, let's face it: my life would be a little easier if Tanana wasn't around.

Tears burn the back of my eyes at my fucked-up logic. What kind of mother am I to even think like this?

Fuck. I need a hit.

"You're thinking about drugs right now, aren't you?"

Damn. I'm not even ashamed that he's right. He needs to just stamp my head with an address and send me straight to hell. "What—are you a mind reader now? You want to try and guess my favorite number?"

I glance at the clock above his head. How much longer do I have to sit here?

"Do you want to pray?"

"For what?"

"For help. For redemption."

I rather pray for a hit.

The good pastor cocks his head. "Our God is a forgiving God. There is no sin too great that he can not forgive."

I don't say anything.

"We all come up short for the glory of God."

Then why bother, I want to shout, but instead I rake my hands through my hair because I still have a half hour of this nonsense to sit through.

"I'm not perfect," he says.

I look at him, remembering the long history I have at this church. Pastor Meyer and his wife have always made salvation sound and look so easy. Just fall on your knees and the kingdom of heaven will open up to you. Just trust in God and he will shower you with expensive Armani suits, rap-star-sized diamonds, and a bright, new, shiny Cadillac every year.

"I see you don't believe me."

No answer.

Pastor Meyer pushes back his chair and stands up and paces the room. "I've met many women like you before in my lifetime. You think your problems are unique or your life choices impossible to overcome."

I shift, feeling uncomfortable again.

"They're not," he says, walking from his desk. "I've helped many women just like you be born again. All you have to do is put your faith in me. Trust that I am a servant of our Lord God. To have favor with me is to have favor with him."

The fever and passion in his voice rises like he's about to kick off one of his Sunday sermons, but there's something different about this one. The message is wrong somehow.

Pastor Meyer stops before me and cups my chin with his large but soft hands and lifts my face until our eyes meet.

"I want to help you," he says with adoring sincerity. "In return for helping you, I need for you to help me."

Just like that, there is a look in his eyes that I recognize.

"Pastor—"

"Shh. Call me Eddie."

My brows lift in surprise.

He only smiles. "If I'm right about you, you're someone who can keep secrets." He waits for his words to sink in. "I know I can keep a secret and we both know God can."

I pull my chin out of his hand and slowly shake my head. "Pastor—"

"Eddie."

"Eddie," I say. "You got this whole thing twisted."

"Do I?" he asks, just as innocent as you please. "Then you don't want this?" He reaches into his pants pocket and removes what can only be described as a gift from God: a nice, long vial of nose candy.

"It's the good shit," he whispers.

My eyes jump back up to his and I swear he looks like the living Messiah to me.

"You want it?" he asks with a sly smile.

I'm nodding without even thinking about it.

"Good." With his free hand, he reaches down and unzips his pants. "There's just one thing you got to do for me first." Before I can react, he crams his four-inch dick into my mouth.

17

Princess

I can't believe she's gone. Dead. She's dead. Lucky . . . is . . . dead.

Seventeen years young.

I am sick of everybody and their supposedly helpful sayings:

"I'm so sorry."

"What a tragedy."

"What a shame."

"God works in mysterious ways."

"It will hurt less with time."

All of it is a bunch of bullshit.

I sit in my windowsill and look out my window across the parking lot at Lucky's bedroom. It hurt like hell that she ain't gone ever be in that window looking back at me. Her funeral is tomorrow. I already have nightmares about her being stabbed, and now I have to go and see her in a casket. Damn. It's only been a week, but it feels like forever. I don't fight the tears.

I don't have the energy to write in my journal. I go to school but my mind ain't there. I just don't give a fuck no more.

My bedroom door squeaks open. "Princess, I'm going to work. You clean up this kitchen before I get home tonight."

I miss Lucky so much that I ache.

"You hear me talking to you?"

"With you yelling how the hell can I *not* hear you," I snap as I pull my knees to my chest.

Since Lucky died I don't have patience for shit.

SLAP!

I gasp as her hand lands on my face and sends my head against the glass of the window. I hold my damn face as I turn and look at her with all the hate I have for her ass in my eyes. I start to tremble. Rage fills me. That volcano that I capped a long time ago finally pops.

I jump up off the windowsill and run at her ass. I use both my hands to push her hard as hell. It feels so good when she stumbles back and falls the fuck on the floor. "Don't put your motherfucking hands on me no damn more," I yell down at her as I ball up my fists.

"No, you didn't put—"

She gets up and I push her ass again. I want to scream at the top of my lungs. My chest feels like it can explode from all them emotions balled up inside of me. Anger. Hatred. Loneliness. Sadness. Fear. Pain. Rage. Murderous Rage. "I'm sick of your shit. I . . . AM . . . SICK . . . OF . . . YOUR . . . SHIT!"

Queen's eyes widen as she looks up at me.

"My best friend is gone. She is dead. She all I had to talk to and tell her about you and your shit. Somebody to believe me. She kept me from going fuckin' crazy around this motherfucker while you sat your fat, man-hungry ass back and let them motherfucking sorry-ass men of *yours* touch me, beat me, *fuck me* and *abuse me!* You no-good bitch, you. Don't you put your fuckin' hands on me no fuckin' more."

Queen pulls herself up to sit on her wide ass as she presses her back to the corner while I bend over and yell in her face the way she did me all these years. The tears and pain flow from me. Years and years of tears and pain.

"You ain't never been no kind of mother to me." I poke my chest. "You ain't shit but a broke pimptress who sold your little girl to *your* men so they can pay these bullshit-ass bills you got."

"That's a lie," Queen spits.

"Don't you ever call me a liar again!" I want to hit her but I don't. I can't. The bitch ain't shit but she is my mother. "I was afraid in my own fuckin' house. Every night I was afraid to go to bed. I was afraid to take a bath. I was afraid to move and draw they attention."

I could hardly see her clearly through the tears I been holding back for so long.

"I did what I had to do to take care of us."

"Shut the fuck up." My voice is soft and tired. She bad as my father, and now I won't call her Momma no damn more. She ain't shit but Queen to me. Enough is enough. I turn away from her to drop down on the edge of the bed. "Just get the hell out my face, *Queen*."

"You not gonna stay in my house and disrespect me after *everything* I gave up for you."

I turn my head to see her as she got up on her feet. I look her dead in her eyes. "No, Queen. I ain't gone stay in your house after *everything* I lost because of you."

She storms toward me and brings her fist down across my nose. I wince in pain as blood spurts against her shirt. She raises her hand to swing again and I jump to my feet to swing on her ass first. I don't think I just react. I give her a nice two-piece right across the chin and in her chest.

"You ungrateful bitch," she spits at me before she grabs my neck with both her hands and pushes me down on the bed. "You think you grown enough to fight me. Huh? Huh? Huh?"

I can't believe she is choking me.

"Your grown ass got just what you was lookin' for," she breathes down into my face like one of them pit bulls or some shit.

And then I just snap. "I hate you for everything you never did for me. I hate you. I hate your ass."

It's all too much.

This confrontation with her.

Lucky's death.

All them years of staying quiet while I was abused by *her* men.

All them years knowing my mother ain't care.

It's just too fucking much. Too much.

I reach up and hit her upside her head with my fists until she releases my throat. I kick her ass off me with both my feet and as soon as she hits the floor I jump dead on that ass.

Everything after that is surreal. It's like standing out of my body watching the shit go down. The blood. The broken furniture. The blue lights of the police. The red lights of the ambulance. Handcuffs. My momma—Queen—on a stretcher. Led out of Bentley Manor by the police. All the shocked eyes on me. Miz Osceola crying while they put me in the backseat of the cruiser.

Jail.

I look around at the small holding cell. It's just like I thought it would be. One toilet. One sink. Two hard plastic benches that are supposed to be beds. It looked like shit and didn't smell much better.

A lady as skinny as me lay balled up on the floor shivering and sweating. She keeps rolling over to throw up on the floor before she rolls back over to keep sweating and shit.

I try not to throw up myself from the smell of her shit. Growing up in the hood, you know a junkie going through a heroin withdrawal when you see one. Most were on crack, but heroin is on the rise, and she's one of its victims. I leave her alone because there ain't a damn thing my young ass can do for her.

I got troubles of my own.

Lucky dead. Queen in the hospital. I'm in jail.

The po-po said I broke her nose and two of her ribs. They say I whupped her ass but I don't remember shit after knocking Queen off of me while she was trying to choke me. I blacked out on her. By the time I came to my senses the police were pulling me off of her.

I look down at the blood smeared on my T-shirt and jeans. Even the soles of my sneakers leave a bloodstained footprint. I reach up and feel my hair. My usual ponytail is gone, and my hair is stuck off in a thousand different directions. My face feels swollen and bruised. I'm sure my mug shot didn't miss none of it.

I'm in Fulton County jail charged with assault and battery. I ain't know if I'm gone get time or what. Probably so. This holding cell ain't shit compared to the real deal. Somebody telling you what to wear, when to eat, sleep, and shit. And even if I do get out, my ass is homeless. Even if I do get out, all the money I saved winning the talent show and working with Danger is hidden in my room back at Queen's. Even if I do get out, I ain't have Lucky to go back to.

Lucky.

Her funeral's tomorrow. It's Friday and I know enough to know my ass is stuck in here for the weekend. I'm gonna miss her funeral.

I slide down to the floor and press my back to the wall as I lay my head against the entrance of the cell. I start breathing all hard and shit. What the fuck have I done? Whupping Queen's ass wasn't worth missing Lucky's funeral.

I drop my head on my knees and cry. I cry like a baby. I cry like the motherless child I am. I cry for Lucky. I cry for my granny. I cry for all the years I sat back quiet while my mother ignored me and *her* men abused me. I cry for fucking up my big chance to record an album with Danger one day.

For all of it.

"Shut up that damn crying," the fiend says weakly from the corner.

But I ignore her.

I'm afraid. Nervous. Anxious. Tired. Beat down and wore down. I'm almost sweating and shaking like that fiend in the corner. What have I done? What the fuck I done did to my life? And God, what the fuck gone happen to me now?

I ain't never felt so cold and alone in all my life.

18

Woo Woo

I'm sitting in my car down the street from the Knight's Inn in midtown. I'm waiting on a call. "Hurry up," I whisper as I smoke another damn Newport like it's going to really calm my nerves. It's a little after two and it takes forty-five minutes to get to my house from here. Friday traffic out of Atlanta is hell. I have to get my ass on the road by four to beat Reggie home from work.

My Akon ringtone sounds off. I jump, nearly dropping my cig onto my new suede Ecko pants. "Yeah," I answer.

"Room 105."

"I'm on the way." I pull out of the parking lot of an abandoned supermarket as I flip my cell phone closed.

In no time I'm parking my Honda in the rear of the hotel back by the funky-ass trash bin. My pulse goes crazy as I pass Hassan's car on my way to the room. Our late-night fuckfests aren't enough for me, but there's no way in hell I will be seen walking in or out of Hassan's apartment during daylight.

I look around me before I open the door and walk into the room. The thick and heavy smell of weed is already in the air. My mouth toots up like it knows I should be smoking, too. Shit, I smoke me some weed on the regular but right now my mind and my pussy is focused on fucking. Straight up.

Hassan is sitting on the foot of the bed in a wifebeater and boxers, flipping through the TV channels.

"You been waiting on this pussy?" I ask him as I pull off my maroon leather trench and let it drop to the floor. My matching sweater and pants drop next until I'm standing there in nothing but a maroon lace teddy with the crotch cut out. This teddy screams: "Ready for action" and "Easy access."

"Get on the bed the way you want me to give you this motherfucker," Hassan orders me as he stands up by the bed.

"You getting right to it, huh?" I ask with a lick of my lips as I climb onto the bed doggy-style. I make sure to wiggle every big inch of my ass the way he likes.

Hassan comes up behind me and puts his hands on my hips to jerk me back to the edge of the bed. "You my nasty bitch?" he asks as he slaps my ass cheeks.

"Damn right I'm your nasty bitch."

"Ask me for it."

He wants me to beg for the long hard dick by our nickname for it. I go right on ahead and give him what he wants. "Give me . . . *The* Dick," I say loud and clear as my whole body tingles in excitement.

I moan as I feel the thick-ass tip snake across my ass before he slaps both my cheeks with it. *WHAP! WHAP! WHAP!*

My pussy jumps to attention, sending my juices down my inner thighs. I'm ready—

"Whoo," I moan as he slips the first thick inch into me.

I slap the bed.

He gives me another inch that I feel spread my moist sugar walls.

I bite the pillow.

He uses his hands to spread my cheeks before he eases his thumb into my ass while he slides the rest of *The* Dick into me with a grunt. "This *my* pussy," he says thickly as he bends over my back to bring his hot hands down to massage my hard nipples. He starts to really ram *The* Dick into me like I stole something.

"Well, Goddamn," I moan as Hassan snatches *The* Dick out of me and then bends over to suck my pussy whole.

"Ah," I cry out roughly as I claw the sheets.

The feel of his tongue on my clit makes hot spasms shoot through my body as I fill his mouth with my cum. I back my ass against his face as he pushes that tongue deep inside me to swirl around like he don't want to miss a damn thing. He shifts up to lick a trail to my ass to circle the hole before he blows cool air against it.

"Ah!" I damn near bite the stuffing out the pillow I'm clutching like a lifesaver.

Still shivering, he flips my ass over on the bed and drops to his knees to run his tongue across my quivering pussy lips. My hips buck up off the bed as he tugs on my swollen clit with his teeth just the way I like.

"Make me cum again, Has," I beg as my upper body flies up off the bed like a knee-jerk reaction. I bring my hands down to tug at his braids as I push his face deeper into my pussy. My clit double pumps like a fired gun as my cum squirts out of me.

"Uhmmmm," he moans as he licks at my pussy like a cat to milk.

My whole body shakes. I cover my face with my hands to keep from screaming.

When Hassan looks up at me, his mouth and chin is wet from my juices. He kisses a hot trail up my body to the valley of my breasts. The feel of his tongue licking at my nipples as he slides about four fingers deep inside me makes me arch my back.

Wanting to please him the way he's pleasing me, I pull at Hassan's beater tee, snatching it over his head to fling away. I push him back against the bed and move down his slender body to push his knees wide apart. I lick my lips and look dead into those sexy-ass green eyes. "Now it's your turn," I say, lowering my head between Hassan's thighs.

I glance at my watch as I jump up out of the bed and hurry into clothes. It's 4:30 p.m. "Shit," I swear.

I drop down to my knees, and the faint mildew of the carpet nearly knocks me over as I look under the bed. Nothing. I get up and lift the covers from the floor and find my teddy on top of Hassan's cotton-stretch boxers.

"You know I'm 'bout sick of this, WooWoo."

I look over at Hassan standing up to pull on his pants as I grab my Louis Vuitton satchel. "Sick of what?" I ask as I reach in the bag for a brush. *See, if I still had my braids I coulda been outta here.*

"Sick of you only wanting to be with me if we fucking sneaking. Sick of you always rushing back to your whack-ass husband. Sick of you not dealing with what you really want and what the fuck your phony ass really is."

"I ain't phony," I tell him with attitude.

"Oh, you ain't?" Hassan snaps.

"And *you* ain't," I shoot back.

We fall silent as I finish trying to brush my hair back into the buster-ass bob Reggie likes me to wear.

"Listen, I love you, WooWoo—"

I turn and wrap my arms around his neck. "And you know I love you, Has."

He locks his hands around my wrists and takes my arms from around his neck. "*But* I don't want to be with you if you got to sneak and shit. I'm sick of eating *Reggie's* pussy. I'm sick of sneaking with *Reggie's* wife."

"So what the fuck you sayin', Has?" I ask as I step back to look at him.

"I'm saying leave your husband and move into my apartment."

Now I know Hassan done lost his motherfucking

mind. I move past him to grab my keys. "You think I'm moving back into Bentley Manor?"

Hassan grabs my arm and twirls me around to step into my face. "What the fuck, you better than me now? You too good for where the fuck you from?"

"Excuse the hell out of me for wanting better. What's sad is your ass don't even see that there is better out there. I ain't ashamed of growing up in the hood. I ain't ashamed of Bentley Manor. Sometimes I miss the hood. I miss Bentley Manor and all my friends and shit, but *damn right* I'm glad to be up outta there. If I'm wrong for that then so the fuck what."

Hassan's face twists in anger and I lean back to look at him. "I'm saying I'm not ready yet. Give me some time. This is a big decision, Has. Way too big for you to be stressin' me for an answer in some dingy-ass hotel room."

"The same dingy hotel your ass wanted to come to 'cause you don't want nobody to know me and you fucking around." The anger leaves his eyes and is replaced with pain. "How the fuck you think this shit make me feel?"

"I'm not trying to hurt you but you knew the situation going in. You act like I blindsided you or some shit—"

"Fuck that. We been dealing for two fucking years. I done had enough of this shit." Hassan pushes me and I fall back into the wall. He grabs his hoodie and his keys before he walks to the door. "When you ready to step up and be a woman 'bout yours, call me. Until then? Just leave me the fuck alone, WooWoo."

He slams out the room and I couldn't do shit but drop down to sit on the end of the bed.

Touch of Class is packed as ever. The smell of bodies, liquor, and the chicken being fried and sold in the back is one of a kind. Only in the dirty South could you party, get your drink on, and get a twelve-pack of fried chicken wings.

It's been a minute since I been to the club, but I'm a bitch on a mission. Nothing or no one can keep me up out of here tonight.

"Let me get a Hpnotiq and Hennessy," I tell the buff-ass bartender as I turn to look around the crowded club.

For as long as I knew Hassan, on Friday nights he'd collect whatever money is owed out to him by his customers and then head out to Touch of Class around twelve. This is the spot to find him, and that's my goal for the night.

Ever since he walked out on my ass in the hotel today, he won't answer my calls to his cell phone. The thought of it really being over is fucking with me big-time. There's no way I can let it go down like this.

So I lied and told Reggie that I was going to Lexi's for a card game. They usually lasted until one or two in the morning. So I'm good for a minute. I have other shit on my mind than Reggie.

"This Is the Way I Live" booms against the walls of the club and the gyrating bodies as I look around for Hassan or his boys. Nothing. I sip on my drink and squeeze my way out the small club to see if his car is even outside.

"Whaddup, WooWoo!"

"Nothing much," I call back to whoever called out to me. I didn't even bother to turn and see who it is. Fuck 'em.

Even the parking lot is crunk as hell. There's enough weed floating in the air to give you a contact. I go right on 'head and breathe it on in.

"Damn, Has. You doin' it like that, son?"

I turn toward the direction of that voice so fast that most of my drink flies out my cup. My mouth drops open. Hassan is twirling some bitch in the front of some-one's car with their headlights on as a crowd of his friends stand around watching and cheering on his show.

It takes a second but I recognize the bitch. It's Candy, some bullshit-ass local celebrity because she was in a few low-level hip-hop videos.

My mouth twists as I take in the strapless jean dress she wore under a leather tight-fitting jacket with leather knee boots. I have to admit that the bitch had a frame that put Buffy the Body to shame. Still, she doesn't make me want to go home and sit in the mirror and ask the Lord why I can't be her. That's a big nothing.

Hassan fucking with Candy? How long *that* shit been going down?

I toss the rest of my drink down and don't even care when some of it splashes on the legs of my new Lucky jeans. My chest feels like a tornado is spinning through it as Candy steps up and wraps her arms around Hassan's neck while he cups her big ass and smacks it.

I'm halfway over there to snatch that bitch when I stop. I can't be out at the club fighting some other bitch over Hassan. I pick up my cell phone and dial his number. I watch as he takes one hand off Candy's jiggling ass to send me straight to voice mail.

19

Woo Woo

Leaving that club last night was one of the hardest things I ever did. At first when Lexi and Reggie started blowing up my cell phone I ignored their calls. I felt like I wasn't going no damn where until I spoke to Hassan. So I sat in the club and watched Hassan and Candy partying it up. Even when he saw I was there he ignored me. All of his time and attention was focused on some video ho.

Around two his ass disappeared. For a minute I didn't see shit but Candy with more video vixen-looking chicks. So I went right back outside and the spot where Hassan's Lexus sat was empty.

While I drove like crazy to Bentley Manor I kept calling his phone and he kept sending my ass to voice mail. I drove into the parking lot of Bentley Manor and couldn't do shit but bang my fist against the steering wheel to see that his car wasn't parked there.

When it looked like my fight with Hassan was gonna have to wait, I went to Lexi's and gave her my cell phone. I told her to hold on to it. She gave me the heads-up that Reggie was looking for me and knew I hadn't been at her house. Oh, a bitch like me is always on the grind. Always. I ain't forgot a damn thing about my hood roots and the hood taught you early to always and forever think fast on your feet.

About a block from our house I pulled on the side of the road. I lugged out my full-sized spare tire and rolled it in some dirt and stones to give it a used look. Next I used a screwdriver to puncture a hole in it before I pressed the air out that motherfucker with my knees. I reached under the flap of the trunk and grabbed the shit people used to change a tire. I opened its case and emptied that into the trunk before I flung the tire on top of it. A little dirt and grime on my knees and hands and just as calm as I fucking please I jumped in my ride.

Reggie bought the flat-tire story, and he bought that I missed and left my cell phone at Lexi's and couldn't call for help. Good. I had other shit on my mind.

My ass ain't sleep all night. And as soon as Reggie left for his half a day at his practice I'm up, dressed, and headed back to Bentley Manor.

I drive through the main gate and circle back out. Sure enough, Hassan's car is parked in its normal spot. The whole time I drive down to the gas station, park my car, and jog back to the complex, my heart is racing like crazy. I come up by the back of the buildings before I cut up to walk into Hassan's.

As I knock on his door, I just tell myself with the utmost seriousness that we are going to get to the bottom of all this shit once and for all.

"So you're just gone sit there fucking with your precious shit like I ain't sitting here?" I ask as I watch Hassan sitting at the kitchen table cutting up his dope to fit into the vials.

He won't say shit. Matter fact he ain't said nothing since he opened the door for me, and that was thirty damn minutes ago. No matter what I say, nothing will get his attention away from that fucking dope:

"So you fucking Candy?"

"I saw you and your video bitch at the club."

"How long you been fucking that bitch?"

"I can't stand your ass."

"Let me get the fuck outta this motherfucker. I'm gone. Bye-Bye."

"So you giving that bitch *The* Dick, too?"

Hassan ignores every damn thing that comes out of my mouth as he sits there in an oversized black tee and jeans. His hair is freshly braided. His angular face all determined and shit as he ignores my ass and focuses on handling his "work."

Another ten minutes goes by with me sitting at the table with my legs crossed wanting to get *something* out of his ass. I stand up and reach across the table to nudge him in the face. "You know what. Fuck you, then. I'm going home to my motherfucking husband—"

Hassan jumps to his feet so fast that the table tilts up, sending the plate holding the dope crashing to the floor. "Go to your husband and keep livin' a fuckin' lie. You think I give a fuck? 'Cause I don't give a fuck, you fake-ass *bitch*," he shouts in my face with veins protruding from his neck as his eyes bulge like he 'bout to stroke the fuck out.

I use both my hands to shove him back away from me. He stumbles and falls against the window. "No, fuck *you*, bitch."

Hassan flexes his shoulders. "Let me give you what you want so you can get the fuck outta here," he says over his shoulder as he stalks into his bedroom.

Not quite sure what the fuck this fool is going for—like his nine millimeter—I run the fuck outta his apartment. Even as I fly down the stairwell I hear him hollering down behind me. "Why you runnin'? This all you want. Come get this motherfucker. Trust me, you can get *this* shit."

I bust outta the door, and I can just shit myself to see people already hangin' around chillin' in the parking lot. "Shit . . . shit . . . shit," I swear as several people, including Miz Cleo and Miz Osceola, look me dead in my face before I can remember to throw up my hood.

I hear the door of the building open and slam close.

"Huh, bitch. This all the fuck you want any motherfucking way!"

I turn and something solid and thick hits me dead in the face, knocking my head back a little bit before it falls to the ground.

"Oh, what the fuck is that?" somebody yells out.

"That looks like a—"

"Damn, Has, you fucking *Woo Woo?*" somebody else asks.

Embarrassment fills me like a motherfucker. My secret is out. Everybody will know. The ghetto gossip delivery service is off the chain. Lexi. Oh, God, somebody going to tell Lexi. Shit. Shit. Shit.

I flip the fuck out in anger and start swinging out on Hassan like he's a fucking stranger to me. I took him by surprise and I can see it on his face. It fuels the fire in me. I feel my fists landing blow after blow, stunning his ass before he gets his shit together and starts swinging back on me. Them licks that motherfucker put on me hurt but I fight back like a fucking soldier until somebody pulled us apart.

Hassan's face is bloody from my nails and my chest feels numb from his blows. My head feels like it's spinning and one of my eyes is already swelling shut.

Hassan starts pacing in the middle of the circle of people surrounding us. "I'm sick of this shit," he hollers, with his hands slicing through the air. "Face facts, bitch, you is what you is. Fuck that."

My mouth drops open as I watch this crazy motherfucker pull his torn T-shirt over his head, exposing the breasts that are strapped down and flattened by duct tape. "I ain't no dude, bitch. I don't give a fuck how I dress or how I walk and fucking talk, you stupid bitch. You eat my pussy just like I eat yours, bitch. You a dyke . . . deal with it."

The gasps of the crowd is like something out a damn movie. Some people knew that crazy-ass Hassan was really a girl. Some people didn't. Damn it, they know now.

I scratch and fight whoever is holding me, trying to get at that motherfucker. "You's a stupid bitch, *Leslie*," I say sarcastically.

Hassan/Leslie walks over to scoop up the strap-on dildo that he threw at me earlier. He puts it to the crotch area and makes the dick bob up and down as the crowd laughs. "Call me Has like you always do when I'm giving you *The* Dick."

He tosses that bitch and the crowd all jumps back. It lands in a puddle of water with a *splash*.

"Damn WooWoo a fucking dyke, yo!"

"Shit, fuck that. Hassan ain't a dude? What the fuck is that shit all about?"

I give Hassan one last nasty stare before I run out of Bentley Manor. People turn to watch me as I run down the street to the gas station and hop into my ride. My hands are shaking so damn bad, and my heart feels like the shit is going to run up out of my chest. I can hardly start the car my hands are shaking so bad, but I know I have to get away from there.

I reverse out the spot.

"Hey!"

I slam on the brakes and turn to look through the back window to see a lady shaking her fist at me. I throw the car into drive and squeal out of the parking lot.

Shit. Damn. Fuck. Bullshit. Motherfucker. Hell. Damn. No. Hell no. Everybody knows. *Everybody* knows.

That shit keeps running through my head as I drive. People blow horns at me as I race through red lights. Even when I turn the corner too close and run up on the curb, I keep driving, ignoring the angry squeal as the front side of the car drags against a metal pole.

I don't know how the hell I make it home in one piece, but as soon as I walk through the front door, I drop to the floor and cry like I just discovered my life is over.

Hey, this is Leesha to some . . . WooWoo to most. Either way, leave me a message.

Beep.

"*Woo, this Lexi. What the hell going on with you and Hassan? All kinds of motherfuckers from Bentley Manor blowing up my phone talkin' 'bout you gay. What the hell were you doing there, anyway? What the hell is going on, Woo? Call me.*"

Beep.

"*Leesha, I'm worried about you, little sister. I'm outside. Come and open the door. I'm not leaving until I know you okay.*"

Beep.

"*WooWoo, this Has . . . I ain't mean for that shit to go down like that today. I was just so shitting at your ass because I love you and you know you love me, too. Shit, it wasn't my business to tell about you being gay on the low or whatever but I ain't gone lie that, I'm glad it's out. Maybe now you'll fucking deal with it and see it ain't that big a deal. You love who you love, Woo. And that's all to it. Just call me.*"

Beep.

"*Leesha, if I have to wait here until Reggie gets home to let me in I will. Open the fucking door, girl.*"

Beep.

"*I meant to tell you there ain't shit going on with me and Candy. I saw you at the club and I pushed up on that bitch just to make you jealous. I swear to fucking God I love you, Woo. I love your ass. You got me crying and shit. I wish I knew where you live 'cause I would come right there and get you and bring you right here where you fucking belong . . . with me.*"

Beep.

"Baby, this me. I'm running a little late but I'll be home by three at the latest. Don't cook. It's Saturday and we'll go to Café Dupree. Love you. Bye."

Beep. Beep. Beep.

I close my cell phone and take the raw steak off my eye. Thank God it isn't black and the swelling went down enough that I can blame it on allergies or something. I already have my lie ready about being in an accident. I step away from the mirror and drop down on the toilet.

If I can only press Rewind and delete this morning. Like I'd really be that fucking lucky.

20

Takiah

Grandma Cleo is at it again.

She's staring me down over breakfast like I'm some damn puzzle she can't figure out or a broken kitchen appliance she can't fix. Hell, you'd think that she'd be happy that I'd finally got a job. Of course the job has been fuckin' her beloved pastor until he's speakin' in tongues for the past month, but she doesn't need to know the details.

Eddie was right: I know how to keep a secret.

"So what do you do down there at the church?" she finally asks while spooning oatmeal to Tanana.

"Just a little bit of everything," I answer, straddling the line of truth. I do perform a little of everything: A little fuckin', a little suckin', and a whole lot of blow.

Shit. I don't know why I didn't pick up on Pastor

Meyer's junkie signs sooner. The sweatin', the wild and watery eyes—it's all right there. Motherfucker has one hell of a hustle going on.

I don't give a shit. I'm gettin' what I need and I'm a better woman for it. Gone are my suicidal thoughts and the daydreams of hurtin' my baby. I'm free to concentrate on doin' what I need to do: savin' this paper Eddie is breakin' me off and tryin' to find my own place, even if it's my own apartment in this hell-hole.

I glance up at Grandma Cleo and she's still staring me down like my ass is suddenly going to break down with a confession.

She should know better than that.

A fierce pounding at the front door startles everyone at the table.

"Who in the hell?" Grandma says, jumping from her chair.

Tanana let loose one of her mighty wails, and I go to take her into my arms when a voice in the hallway stops me in my tracks.

"Takiah, is yo ass in there?"

Kameron.

"Oh, shit." My heart tries to crack its way through my chest. I snatch Tanana out of her chair and look wildly around for a place for us to hide.

"You stay right there," Grandma Cleo instructs firmly and then marches toward the front closet door. "I'll handle this."

"Grandma, no," I warn her. Kameron is a nigga not to be fucked with, and he can certainly take a seventy-one-year-old church lady down with no problem.

"You heard what I said."

"Takiah," Kameron roars. "Open this goddamn door! I know yo triflin' ass in there!"

Grandma Cleo ignores her infamous Louisville Slugger and instead withdraws an impressive-sized gun from the top shelf.

When in the hell did she start packin' that thing?

Despite Tanana's bawlin', I clutch her tighter while feeling rooted to the floor. This is all my fault. I shoulda been more prepared for this moment, and now that it's here . . . what?

The banging continues, and when Grandma Cleo's hand lands on the doorknob, I call out one more warning, but she seems not to need it.

In the next second, Grandma Cleo jerks open the door and aims her gun directly into Kameron's enraged face all in one fluid motion. I'm surprised, but Kameron is completely thrown off his game.

It's the first time I've seen his face since I'd lit his

ass up, and let me tell ya, he ain't so pretty no more. He looks like something that crawled out of a nightmare. His once smooth, chocolate skin is now splotchy pink, tight and shiny and looks like it still hurts like hell.

"Whoa, old lady." Kameron tosses up his hands like he's just been surrounded by police. "Calm down. I just wanna holla at my wife for a sec," he says all calm and diplomatic-like.

"Sounded like you was hollering at the whole damn building," Grandma Cleo chastises, keeping her aim steady. "And your wife doesn't have nothin' to say to you."

Kameron's eyes narrow and I can feel his fury from across the apartment. "Look, old lady. I don't wanna hurt you."

"And I don't wanna shoot you . . . but I will if you don't get away from my door and leave me and my family alone."

"Look." He licks his thick lips. "She got my daughter with her."

I hug Tanana tighter and try to quiet her by bouncing her on my hip while Grandma coldly looks Kameron over.

"Baby don't look nothing like you," she tells him.

It's the first time someone vocalized what Kameron

and I both know. Tanana isn't his child, and only God really knows who her daddy is.

"Look," he tries again.

However, he's worn out Grandma Cleo's patience, and she quickly points the gun to the floor and fires off one round and then points the gun back at his face as fast as any quick draw from the Old West.

"I said 'get.' "

Kameron lifts his head and his hands higher, but there's a calculating look in his eye. Is he really foolish enough to try and push his luck?

"Is there a problem, Cleo?"

Miz Osceola's voice drifts in from the hall, and I can tell by the sudden stiffness in Kameron's frame that another gun was now pointed at his back.

"No trouble," Grandma says calmly. "This young man was just leavin'. Weren't ya?"

I swear if looks could kill, Grandma would be goin' on to meet her beloved Jesus. I somehow feel like I'm sort of watchin' all of this like it's a damn movie of the week until Kameron's eyes slice toward me with a promise that nearly stops my heart.

"Weren't ya?" Grandma asks again.

Kameron finally pulls his eyes away from mine and gives Grandma Cleo what I think is a smile. "Yes, ma'am. I was just leaving."

Slowly, he turns from the door, and I finally collapse in the nearest chair and wait for my heart to return to its regular rhythm.

I had a long wait ahead of me.

Later that night after Bible study, Eddie and I snorted a few lines in his office to jump off our little late-night party. Despite being high as a kite, I still can't get Kameron's monstrous face out of my head.

"I think he's going to kill me," I whisper.

The good pastor takes another long snort and then tilts his head all the way back on the leather couch. "Who?" he asks, unzipping his pants.

"My husband."

Eddie's hand stills on his crotch as his eyes pop open. "Your husband? I thought he was in jail—in D.C."

"Well, apparently he got out."

"What? He came here?" He sits up, looking around, paranoid. "Is he dangerous?"

"No. Shit, I don't know. He could be on his way back to D.C. for all I know. Grandma Cleo warned him off pretty good."

"Aw, well, hell. If Cleo handled it, we don't have to

worry," Eddie boasts, pulling out his small-ass dick and gliding my head down to get on my job.

I ain't crazy about doin' this shit 'cause a bitch can get lockjaw tryin' to get his limp, needle dick hard. Yeah, he does a bunch of moanin' and pumpin' his hips, but gettin' his ass to cum is a whole 'nother story.

The only weird thing is how he gives thanks every couple of seconds while I'm gettin' him off. I'm suckin' and slurpin' and all I hear is, "Thank you, Jesus."

When he *finally* cums it's: "Hallelujah. Hallelujah."

Whatever. I got my blow. I got my money. He can take my ass home now.

"How was Bible study?" Grandma Cleo asks before I get into the door good.

"Fine," I answer, avoiding her gaze.

Silence and then, "It sure is nice of Pastor Meyer helpin' you out like he is."

"I guess." I peel off my coat.

"Have you given your life over to God yet?"

I can't help but roll my eyes. "Grandma, you said I had to go to counseling or get out. I'm going. You said I needed to get a job. I got one. Is there something else you want me to do that I'm not doin' good enough for you?"

"You can check that tone," she snaps. "You know I don't abide by none of that nonsense. If you're living here, you're goin' to give me the proper respect."

"Yes, ma'am."

"I'm just asking you some questions. That's all. There's been some talk lately."

"What kind of talk?"

She hesitates. "Just some stuff I ain't wantin' to believe."

"Then don't believe it," I say, bored with the conversation. I'm too tired for this shit. "I'm goin' to bed." I can tell there's something else she wants to say, but she chooses not to say it. Thank God.

By the next morning, I don't feel too good. The moment I climb out the bed, I'm racing to the bathroom and doubling over, vomiting in the toilet. I don't eat much and therefore I don't have much to let go. In a matter of seconds my belly cramps from dry heaving.

When I'm finished, I'm not surprised to see Grandma wrapped in her robe and filling up the bathroom doorframe.

"Lawd have mercy. Chile, tell me you ain't pregnant."

21

Princess

Two months and seventeen hours.

That's how long I spent locked up by the Fulton County sheriff's department. That's one thousand, four hundred and fifty-seven hours or eighty-seven thousand, four hundred and twenty minutes. If time was money, I'd be straight. And if time was love, then I wouldn't feel so damn alone and scared as I stand outside the jail and try to figure out what the hell to do with myself now that I'm free.

That Monday after I was locked up, the magistrate gave me a $2,000 bond. Without any money or any help to get the money, it might as well been a million dollars. I thought I might get something called a PR bond, but Queen came testifying that she was scared of me and didn't want me back to her house. Damn, will she ever stop hurting me?

Because I was seventeen about to turn eighteen, the cops didn't even think about transferring me to juvenile detention. I had to stay on lock while I waited for my trial date. So here I am looking at a year for my charge and trying to learn to get used to life in jail. Eat now. Sleep now. Out your cell. In your cell. Lights out. Lockdown. Count. Shit here. Wash there. Do this. Don't do that.

What's crazy is there's some really cool people in jail. I didn't make no friends, but I didn't make no enemies in that crowded and pissy motherfucker either. Some people I will remember; most I will forget.

I went to court early this morning and coulda pissed my pants when they gave me two years straight probation and a thousand-dollar fine. The probation wouldn't have been that bad, but I didn't realize in that commotion I broke a chair on Queen. That took a simple assault and battery to a whole 'nother level.

When they finally finished up my paperwork or whatever they was doing that took all day, there wasn't a soul waiting to hug me and be happy for me and to take me home. When I did try to call Queen collect, she denied the charges.

I'm on my own. I'm free to be homeless and penniless . . . but not hopeless. I can't let myself give up. I have to make it. I *have* to.

It was mid-December and Georgia or no Georgia it's cold. The wind whips and bites through the short-sleeved T-shirt I'm wearing. I shake off any sadness or feeling bad for myself as I start walking up Rice Street. I notice people staring at me.

I can't really blame them.

When they took back the jail uniform, I had to put on the same bloody clothes I had on when they locked me up. It's not like I had anybody to bring me something different. It isn't a lot of blood, but it's enough smeared on my shirt and jeans—especially without a overcoat to cover it—to make me look crazy as hell.

I dig my shivering hands down into my pockets to hold the last ten dollars I have to my name. In my other pocket I wrap my hands around the piece of folded paper my public defender gave to me. I reach for it.

I never thought I would be in this situation, but I'm homeless and I damn sure need shelter. I unfold the paper to look down at the address and directions. A Helping Hand is just a five minute walk from here. I have to get there in time to get one of the hundred beds they have available for the night.

I tuck my head to my chest and take off walking as fast as I can as the wind seems to fight me every damn step of the way.

The line for the shelter is reaching the corner when I get there, but I stand there freezing, my teeth chattering, hoping I ain't too far back in line to get a bed. "Please, God, look out for me," I pray as I huddle against the wall.

God is definitely on my side, because I get the second to last spot and I have to force myself not to damn cry. I learn something about the goodness of people as they give me a used purple sweatsuit to put on. It makes me look like a dried-up Barney, but it's clean and I don't have to walk around looking like a murder suspect. I don't throw the bloody outfit out. Hopefully with a good washing at the Laundromat, most of the blood will come out, and these clothes would be good to go for more wear.

Ain't like I had shit else. All my shit is at Queen's, but as soon as I get myself together I will go straight to the police and go get my clothes and hopefully the little bit of money I have stashed away.

After a hot shower and an even hotter meal of beef stew and cornbread, we are led into two small rooms painted the color of baby doo with about fifty cots in each one. There isn't much room to walk, and the room is crowded with women and children who are either playing loudly or crying loudly.

It's the best noise I ever heard.

I make my way over to a cot at the end of the row by the wall and sit my plastic bag on it. It's a damn shame when you hold on to prison toiletries 'cause you don't have shit else in the world to call your own.

I notice a thirty-something white woman with a one-year-old eyeing me from the bunk next to me. I smile at her and look away.

"Hi, I'm Halle and this is Angel," she says, obviously taking my smile for an opening.

"I'm Jamillah but everyone calls me Princess."

"Nice to meet you."

I don't really say much more. I just want to lay down and chill. Get my thoughts together. Make some damn plans.

I turn on my side, putting my back to her as I stare at the shit-colored walls. My eyes are just starting to close when little Angel starts whining and crying inconsolably. I wonder how I will ever have kids of my own when I'm so scared of men. The only man I ever crushed on had a sexy girlfriend that I can't hardly compete with. Besides, who knows if I will ever see Danger again? And that meant my chance at a record deal is like the rest of my life. Shot to hell.

Needing a distraction, I turn over and sit up on the edge of the bed. My knees nearly touch Halle's as I smile into Angel's big watery eyes and sing "Hush Little Baby" real soft for her ears only.

Soon she begins to coo and then root around on her mother's chest before her head falls back over her mother's arm like a passed-out drunk.

Halle reaches over to grab my wrist. I jump back from her touch and she pulls her hand away with a smile filled with apologies. She turns to lay the baby on her stomach in the middle of the cot. "Thanks so much. She always goes through this crying fit before she goes to sleep."

"You're welcome." I lie back down, wanting to get back in my alone zone.

"You look really young," she says.

"I just turned eighteen." I try to sound all hard so she'll leave me alone.

"I just turned thirty myself—"

I look at her over my shoulder. "Listen, Halle, no offense, but I got a lot going on right now and I just want to rest my eyes and get myself together, you know?"

She looks hurt and offended, but she just nods as she focuses on rubbing her baby's back.

I don't feel good about dissing her, but I do have a bunch of drama in my own life, and my brain just can't take getting filled up with somebody else's story. Hell, it's not like she has a good one to tell, since she in the shelter with my ass.

About an hour later, I hear Halle singing to Angel in an off-key voice. She can't sing a lick, but her version sounds much better than mine because her voice is filled with a mother's love.

I turn over on my stomach and watch her through half-closed eyes. She's lying on her side looking down at her baby as she rubs her back and sings to her. I can tell she loves her daughter, and it makes me wonder if there was ever a time that Queen loved me. Maybe as a baby she had held me close and rocked me when I cried. Maybe?

Tears fill my eyes. "Hey, Halle, can I tell you something I wish someone had told my mother?"

She looks up at me, and I can see that she doesn't know how to take me. "Sure."

"Whenever you do get on your feet and get your own place please be careful of the men you bring into her life, because they can change her life in the worst ways you can imagine. They won't look like perverts and kid beaters but some will be and they can fill her with memories and nightmares she won't ever outrun.

Put your child first. Always. Make sure she don't go through what the fuck I been through."

Halle looks like she wants to say something, but she closes her mouth as she nods at me again. I turn over and hug my thin bleach-smelling pillow close as I cry quietly. I'm sure she has questions. Wanted answers. Needed explanations.

Thank God she just left me the hell alone.

The next afternoon I drop my plastic bag onto the cold ground before I kneel beside the grave. I reach out and trace the grooves of Rendell "Lucky" Hunt.

Like most other shelters, we were given breakfast, but no one is allowed to lounge all day on the premises. Even though I knew I had to find a job, I had to come here first. I had to.

At first the words won't come. I just sit there reminiscing on the years of friendship we shared that wasn't hardly enough. It has been so long since I really talked to anyone. I just been holding it all in. All of it. But I eventually take a deep breath to calm myself, and the words flow like water.

How good it felt to whup my momma's ass.

How bad I felt about whupping my momma's ass.

How scared I was when I got locked up.

How glad I am to be free.

How scary it is to be free but homeless and penniless.

The bullshit party some of the girls in prison threw for my birthday.

How much I loved that bullshit party, because it was the only party anybody ever threw for me.

How much it hurt me when she died.

How much I miss her.

How afraid I am.

How lonely I am.

"Lucky, I need you to watch out for me from heaven 'cause I ain't got nobody else out here on these streets. It's just me, myself, and I. Right now I can use all the help I can get."

22

Woo Woo

It's been a couple of weeks since that shit went down at Bentley Manor, and I ain't been back since. Hassan is still calling me, but I'm not answering him . . . her . . . whatever. I'm more determined than ever to make my marriage work. I have to be. Hassan and I will never work.

I roll over in bed and give Reggie a kiss on his shoulder before I climb out of bed.

"Leesha—"

"WooWoo," I say suddenly as I look down at him like I can really see him in the darkness.

"Huh?"

"When you married me I was WooWoo. You even called me WooWoo. Nobody ever calls me by my real name and sometimes I forget you talkin' to me. For real," I tell him with honesty.

"Okay, whatever. *WooWoo*, where you going?" he asks with a tinge of attitude.

"I just want to sit up and look at the tree for a little bit."

He doesn't say a word. I knew he wouldn't. Since I've been hanging right under him recently, he hasn't had too many questions for me.

I grab my robe—*Oh God, I wear a fucking robe*—and walk out the room. "Reggie?" I call out to him as I stop at the door.

"Huh, baby?" he asks, sleepily.

"When you married me I was ghetto as hell. Long nails, smoking weed, cussing and fussing with braids down to my ass. You still married me, right?"

He hesitates before he answers. "Right."

"Then I don't see why you wanted me to change when we got married. Sometimes I look in the mirror and wonder who the fuck that lady is I'm looking at."

I turn on the bedroom light before I walk back over to the bed.

Reggie pulls a pillow over his head as he groans. I reach right down and pull it from his face. "Wasn't nothing wrong with me before," I tell him, feeling weight lift off my shoulders.

He looks up at me. "I didn't say there was."

I nod as I smile down at him. "Good, because this Suzie Homemaker shit stops today. The braids are going back in. My nails are going back long and I'm gone be WooWoo. Leesha's ass is gone."

He looks at me for a long-ass time. "Where all this coming from?"

"Just some shit that been on my chest for a minute. I decided to get it off."

"I'll say like you say. You tripping."

"It's trippin', not tripping," I correct him with a slap to his ass.

"Look, WooWoo, Leesha, Sybil, whoever you are tonight. I love you. I would prefer the way you look now but I will love your crazy ass regardless of how you wear your hair and your nails. I had a preference but I never gave you an ultimatum. If you feel like you weren't true to yourself then blame yourself, baby . . . not me."

I cross my arms over my chest. "So you wouldn't be ashamed of me as your wife?"

Reggie sits up in bed and reaches up to pull my hand. I fall into bed beside him. "I'm not gone lie and say you know you shouldn't demonstrate your ability to belch for a full ten seconds at a dinner party, but I know you know how to handle yourself in any situation. I married you, *Woo Woo*. I love you, *Woo Woo*. And I'm so happy with you, *Woo-Woo*."

I tilt my head up to kiss him.

"Can I go back to sleep now?" he asks as he playfully slaps my ass.

I climb out of bed. My thoughts are so heavy. I'm so damn confused. So fucked up.

I already knew that he loves me. I know it, but I just wish I can say I love him just as much.

I give him one last look before I turn out the lights and leave the room.

Fuck the hair and nails. Even when I change those back to the WooWoo everybody used to know, I'm still not being true to me and what I want. Or what I think I want? Sometimes what you want ain't what you need, but you want it bad.

I walk into the den where we put one of our three Christmas trees in the house. Reggie knows how much I love this holiday, and he went above and beyond to make our first one something I'd never forget. This tree with the big colorful balls and flashing lights is my favorite. It's more like me. Wild and loud.

And I do love Christmas. It was the only time of the year that my cracky-ass momma would at least try to do right. She usually did good until early evening, when she would find any excuse to get out the door and hit the streets. Our grandma would give us so much love that she hoped me and Lexi wouldn't be hurt when Momma dipped. It didn't work, but we loved our grandma more for trying.

I can't help but wonder what she would think if she knew about my relationship with Hassan. Lexi still trippin'. She's not mad or nothing, just shocked. Sexy WooWoo, who always screams about being "strictly dickly," is . . . is . . .

What? Gay? Bi? A Freak?

All I do know is that I fell for Hassan, but the fact remains that *he* is really a *she* named Leslie. I just didn't know that when he moved into Bentley Manor two years ago. Something about the light-skinned cutie drew me away from Reggie. In Hassan I found all the things I knew Reggie would never understand. Do. Be. I loved Reggie and our relationship, but there was something about Has that drew me right on in. Still, I can't help but wonder if I had known the truth about Hassan from the start if that door inside of me would have ever been opened. . . .

Hassan and I had already been flirting hard with each other when he invited me up to his apartment that first time. I was so excited to finally spend some alone time with him that my panties were creamy when I climbed the stairwell from my first-floor apartment to his on the second.

I knock. He opens the door. We stare at each other hotly before he reaches for my hand and pulls me inside. He leads me to the futon over by the window. I pick up the blunt already blazing atop a beer can on the crates he's using for a coffee table. He has a bottle of Henney and I reach for it to take a deep sip.

For the next thirty minutes we just get fucked up as we talked about shit we had in common. Shit my boyfriend Reggie wouldn't even understand. Music. Types of weed. Clothes style. Food. TV shows.

I tilt my head back to blow smoke rings to the sky. I don't say shit when I feel his hot hands moving up my bare legs to squeeze my thick thighs and push my short jean skirt up around my waist. I'm so horny and ready for that dick. He had that lean and slender look I like with angular features. His laid-back style drew me in and made we want to know more about that new kid with green eyes. "Damn, right," I tell him huskily as I spread my legs wide as they can go. "Play in my pussy."

Hassan slips his fingers past my sky blue panties and pushes them deep inside me. I work my hips against his hand.

Finally, I'm thinking, just knowing how lean men usually have big old dicks. I been wanting to have some of him since I first laid eyes on him. I'm not giving up a good thing like Reggie but a little dick on the side won't hurt a thing. What Reggie don't know won't hurt him.

Hassan leans over to press his lips down on mine. Our tongues touch briefly and then we both moan as we deepen it. He lifts my shirt and bra to suck at my nipples like a pro. It's absolutely right. Perfect. The best.

Wanting to feel him, I move to lift his shirt. He helps me snatch it over his braided head before he presses me down onto the futon with his body. His lips search out and find my nipples again.

"Oh, Has—"

My eyes pop open at the feel of his own set of soft breasts against mine.

I jerk his head up with both of my hands. "You're a girl?" I ask, shocked as hell.

He nods and my hands try to stop him

*from working my panties down over my hips.
"I thought you knew. I ain't trying to hide it
or nothing."*

"But . . ."

*I push my hands against his shoulders as
he jerks his head away from my hands to shift
downward.*

*I scoot away. "I'm not gay. I didn't know
you were a fucking girl," I say, scrambling to
get away from the feel of those hands—her
hands—on my body.*

*I always been one of those chicks that
swore up and down they would slap any lesbo
that ever stepped to me. So I am beyond shot
the fuck out that my body is battling how I
thought I would react in a situation like this.*

I still feel excited.

I'm still horny as hell.

Actually I'm not even all that disgusted.

*I'm not fighting that hard to get up. Lips
kiss me intimately there and I don't do shit
but spread my legs wider. . . .*

From then on Hassan and I been sneaking. It's like
wanting something you feel is bad but not being able
to turn it down. It feels like an addiction.

But now I can't lie to myself that I don't love Hassan, because I do. This whole time we've been apart, I've been missing him like crazy. But it was so much easier to be with him when I could fool myself into thinking he was a boy. I could fool myself into thinking my ass wasn't gay or bisexual.

I know the real reason I married Reggie was to prove to myself that I preferred a man. I tried at first to stay away from Hassan. I really tried, but just like now my heart, my soul, and my body craves him like crazy.

I'm not ready to live an open lesbian lifestyle, and now I know Hassan is sick of us sneaking. So that leaves me with one helluva question.

Do I give up my good life with my husband, or move back to the hood with Hassan?

23

Takiah

Christmas is in two days and like all churches, the congregation is treated to a Christmas program by the youth ministry. Young, earnest faces stumbled through unmemorized scripts; however, the children still manage to captivate everyone in their pews. Hell, even I'm moved to tears when baby Jesus (a bundled plastic doll) is finally born in the manger and the cast breaks out in a heart-tugging rendition of "Oh, Come All Ye Faithful."

Faith. That's the last thing I have in this world, but I have to admit: I admire those who do. Not fake-ass Christians like Pastor Meyer and even most of the people sittin' next to me, but like Grandma Cleo.

I steal a quick glance at her and I wonder how she does it. Life has served her one raw deal after another, and she just keeps on praying and keeps on believing that there's some great invisible being in the sky, waiting to shower her with unearthly riches.

Even with her suspicions of what's truly goin' on with me and the pastor, she still shows up, praises Jesus anyway, and keeps on keepin' on about her business.

"I don't put my faith in man," she said the other night. "And when it comes down to it, Pastor Meyer is just a man. You'll do good to remember that."

Yes, he's just a man. A man givin' me what I need for the moment. I can't ask for much more than that.

Honestly? It just all sounds silly to me. I mean, if you're up there, why all the secrecy?

I chance another look at her, and as a result I'm crushed by a wave of sadness. I really do wish I could be like her. I wish I could believe.

I need to believe in something, because I don't know how in the world I'm going to be able to raise *two* babies. At the moment, I'm lying out my ass to my grandma about being pregnant, but I know she doesn't believe me. I know I'm a big disappointment to her, and I wish I could just stop fuckin' up.

But it's the only thing I know how to do.

At least this time, I know who the baby's daddy is.

I twitch through the rest of church service and

pretend I don't hear a few whispers here and there. Due to the holidays, Eddie has been real busy, and my job has been temporarily suspended. I have to figure out a way to get him alone. I got to break the news to him.

However, at the end of service, the pastor is surrounded by different members and genuine church employees that I don't get my chance.

I'll try later, when Grandma and Miz Osceola drag me back for evening service. I can already imagine what he's gonna say.

"Get rid of it!" Pastor Meyer removes a stack of cash from his office safe and slaps it on the corner of his desk like it was the final judgment of a murder case. I guess in a way, it is. "I don't care who, where, or how. Just get rid of it."

I stare at the money. There has to be a few thousand there. More than enough to do what he's asking and pack my shit and get the hell on. This time, to someplace Kameron won't think to look for me.

"What? You need a little bit more?" Eddie asks, watching my greedy gaze and then adding another stack of money. "Of course, if I give you this, I expect this whole problem to go away."

He means me.

Apparently the whispers have finally reached him, too. That, or he's already found my replacement. I suddenly feel sorry for Mrs. Meyer, though I've never given her much thought before today.

"Sure. Okay," I say, reaching for the money. However, the moment my hand lands on top of what feels like my lottery winnings, Pastor Meyer's hand covers mine to stop me.

"Now this doesn't mean that we can't party one last time." With his free hand, he cups one side of my face.

What the fuck am I supposed to say?

"Let's just put this back in the safe and go on over there and tell your grandma that I'll be takin' you home tonight."

That doesn't sound like a good idea.

"We'll tell her that you'll be helpin' me finalize the plans for the church's volunteers to visit the homeless shelters tomorrow. Tomorrow is Christmas Eve, after all."

She might buy that, but I'm willing to bet my life she doesn't.

Then again, what can she say? I'm grown. And the kind of money I can walk out of here with tonight will make it all worth it. Hell, I might not even go home tonight. Make this money, buy a plane ticket, and get the fuck out of Dodge.

Tanana is better off with Grandma Cleo anyway. I don't know shit about raising babies. What kind of life can I offer her?

We leave his office just as the evening's guest pastor is finishing up his sermon and the collection plates have made their way up to the altar for him to bless.

I find the whole thing just . . . sad.

"Who else is working late with y'all," Grandma Cleo asks when I feed her Pastor Meyer's line.

"I don't know," I lie. "He said he was having a hard time getting people to stay committed this close to the holidays."

"Well, I can stay and help him," Miz Nosceola volunteers, settling her hands on her hips. "I ain't got much to do tonight."

"That's not necessary," I tell her, trying to pretend that she's not riding my last nerve.

"Why not? You said he needs help and I'm offering to help."

"But I'm the one that needs the extra money," I tell her. "If you jump in and it takes us less time to do what needs to be done then that's less money for me and Tanana," I lie expertly.

Miz Nosceola purses her lips and turns up her nose, like she smelling something again.

Fuck her. I got to make this money.

Grandma Cleo says nothing, she just looks . . . disappointed. The same look she always has. When she turns to leave the church, my eyes fall on my baby girl, who's hanging on her great-grandma's hip and staring at me like she knows the deal.

Suddenly I'm that five-year-old girl again, watching my mother walk out of my life for good. For the first time, I understand my mother's choices. She left me because she couldn't take care of me.

Now I'm about to do the same thing to my baby girl.

I continue to stare long after Grandma reaches her Lincoln Town car, strap Tanana in her car seat, and then drive out the church's small, pothole-riddled parking lot.

I mope my way back to the pastor's office while he and the other church members talk and they thank him for this evening's service.

I'm actually alone for quite a while, and I start thinking about my life. I mean, *really* thinking about it. As my eyes dart around Pastor Meyer's incredibly clean and organized office, my gaze also falls to the different crucifixes hanging on the wall.

For God so loved the world that he gave his only be-gotten son that whosoever believeth in him should not perish but have everlasting life.

I can't count how many times I've heard that passage from the Bible, and I don't understand why it's ringing in my head now or even why tears are flowing from my eyes.

For God did not send His son to condemn the world, but that the world through Him might be saved.

Finally my eyes land on a picture of Jesus, not the blond hair, blue eyes version, but one of darker skin and kinkier hair, and I find myself asking it the question: "Even me, Lord?"

While I'm waiting for an answer, Eddie bursts through his office door, looking both tired and anxious. "We don't have much time, I told my wife I'd be home before eleven."

As he heads toward the safe, I jump up from the couch, not believing what I'm about to do.

"I can't do this."

Eddie stops and glances at me from over his shoulder. "You can't do what?"

"This," I say, splaying open my hands. "The drugs, the sex . . . the abortion. I-I just can't."

"What, you got a motherfuckin' conscience now?"

His sudden deep, trembling baritone surprises me

and I suddenly feel like I'm standing before my quick-tempered husband who's about to launch over that desk and whup my ass.

"I better go." I pick up my purse and rush toward the door, but old pastor has a little speed on him, and he actually beat me to the door.

"Whoa. Whoa." His big froglike eyes grow even wider. "I thought we had an understanding here." Beads of sweat magically appear and dot across his forehead. "I got a lot on the line here."

"I've changed my mind. I just want to go home."

"You've changed your mind?" He stares at me while the muscles along his jaw twitch. When I don't respond, he laughs and convinces me of one thing: this motherfucker is crazy.

I reach for the doorknob and try to yank open the door, but Eddie is having none of that. "Hold up. Hold up, Sister Takiah. I think we need to sit down and talk about this some more. There's no way in hell I'm about to let you have this baby."

"I'll take the bus home or call a cab," I tell him, still wanting to get out of this office.

"Did you hear what I said?" He sounds demonic, and one look in his eyes tells me if I don't start saying what he wants to hear, I may not ever make it out of this office alive.

"You're right," I say, smiling. "I don't know what I was thinking. I can't take care of no two babies."

He stares me down, judging if I've really come around.

"I just probably need to relax a little," I continue, sliding my hands around his wide waist and then dipping a couple of fingers below his belt. I may be a fuckup, but I'm also a survivor.

A small smile finally curls Eddie's lips. "I think I have just the thing you need." He takes my hand, making sure I don't make a dash out the door, and leads me back over to his safe.

I smile patiently and follow. He doesn't take out the money, or even coke. On tonight's menu is smack. My fingers instantly go to the tracks on my arms. Damn, it's been more than three months since I had some of this shit.

"Ah. I see you want some," he laughs, certain that he's finally won me over.

I'm not so sure that he hasn't.

"Why don't I fix you up first?" he asks.

I try to shake my head, but I smack my lips instead.

"After all, you need to relax a little bit, right?"

I am a little tense, I reason with myself. I know I should stop him. I know I should be thinking about the baby inside of me, but instead I find myself wishing that he would hurry up and fix the shit. Within seconds, a spoon, cotton balls, rubber bands, and new syringes litter his beautiful desk, and I'm quickly rollin' up the sleeve of my dress.

He swabs the bend in my arm, and my gaze falls back to the picture of Jesus. At the same time, the needle punctures my vein.

For God so loved the world that He gave his only begotten son that whosoever believeth in Him should not perish but have everlasting life.

I sob.

For God did not send His son to condemn the world, but that the world through Him might be saved.

"Even me, Lord?" I whisper as Pastor Meyer lifts up my dress. "Even me, Lord?" When I close my eyes and spread open my legs, I finally hear a voice—an answer.

Yes, my child. Even you.

24

Takiah

"Dear Lord, I repent of my sins. I ask you to come into my heart and wash me with your blood. You are my Lord and Savior . . ."

"What? What are you saying?" Pastor Meyer stops stroking his blubbery butt against my boney frame to peer down at me.

I'm so high, I don't even know where we are. I look around, try to concentrate, but my brain just feels like a mushy mess. But I know that for the first time in my life I was talking to God.

And I was happy.

Suddenly, I don't know why I ever doubted he existed. Flashing back through my life, I now know that he has always been there. It was His shoulder I cried on when my mother left me. It was Him who helped me graduate from school and accomplished my first goal of moving out of Bentley Manor. Even when I started making bad choices, He was still there.

He was the one who'd put me on that bus back to Atlanta without me thinking about calling Grandma Cleo first. And He was here now, claiming victory over the devil on top of me.

I smile, but Pastor Meyer thinks the smile is for him, and he returns to stroking and wiggling his small penis inside of me.

I'm in a car, I realize. Eddie's car. I remember now. He wanted to do it one last time before he took me home, and I was too high to protest, too limp to care. I still lack the strength to push him off or to stop what's going on. I just want to close my eyes and go back to talking with God.

Then, like out of some horror movie, a monster appears in the window above me. A scarred brown and pink face twisted into an animal snarl.

"Kameron," I say as a weak alarm.

Pastor Meyer must not have heard me, because in the next second, a cascade of broken glass showers down on us and the passenger door is jerked open.

"What the—?"

Kameron grabs the pastor by the back of his expensive suit and yanks him out. "Motherfucker, don't you know you got to pay to play? I own this bitch."

I scramble to get up just as I hear my husband's fist pound into the fleshy pastor and it's met with a moan of pain that only intensifies when the second strike hits.

"Please, God. Stop. I didn't know," Eddie is saying as I make my way over to the driver's side.

The keys aren't in the ignition.

"Where the fuck you think you're going?"

I whip my head toward my husband at the open passenger door and finally let out a scream when he dives into the car after me. Jerking on the car handle, I spill out onto the hard pavement. Kameron manages to lock one hand around my left ankle.

I scream again, kicking for freedom and ignoring the pain of my naked flesh being dragged across the blacktop.

"C'mon, baby. Don't be like that. We've got some unfinished business we need to discuss."

Before he can pull me up farther, I kick out with my right foot and make a solid connection against his slim nose. I hear as well as feel it crack. This time, he roars in pain, but at least he releases his grip on my ankle. I waste no time with my immediate freedom, turning and jetting into the night with nothing but a few orange-hued streetlights illuminating my path.

I see the rocks, trash, and broken glass littered across the pavement, but I don't feel them as they scratch, puncture, or stab my bare feet, just as I don't register the night's cool breeze against my naked flesh. I have to get away.

My hearing is another matter.

The rushing wind sounds like an ocean's roar, my heart like a ticking bomb, but the city street is eerily silent. Where are all the cars, buses, people?

I'm waiting for the sound of my husband's heavy footfalls—expensive mall sneakers slapping the street. But they don't come. What I hear instead is the roar of a car engine and then the screech of balding tires.

My stride slows for a second, just long enough for me to glance over my shoulder and see the headlights beam from Kameron's Buick.

Terror, like I had never known, seizes my limbs and I stumble. Miraculously, I regain my balance, hike up my knees, and accelerate my speed.

"Hey, look over there." A stranger's voice reaches my ears, and my gaze follows the sound to two figures exiting a convenience store.

"Help," I screech.

But they don't move, frozen, gawking at the scene unfolding.

My racing thoughts clear out the rest of the drug-induced fog, and snapshots from my short life start to flash in my head, the pictures speeding up until it's like watching a movie. Suddenly, all my mistakes and poor choices are so glaringly obvious.

God had given me so many chances to turn my life around. Wasted chances. A wasted life.

Grandma Cleo swept through my mind. I'm sorry for the permanent lines of disappointment that I've carved in her tired face, but still marvel at the love that she still gave me. And I'm overwhelmed by the love I suddenly feel for her.

Tears flow down my face when I remember the first time the hospital nurse placed Tanana in my arms. Instead of thanking God for the miracle of ten fingers and ten toes, I'd thought I'd delivered a bur den. A complication I didn't need or want. Now there was nothing in the world I wouldn't give to have her in my arms again.

"I'm so sorry, baby," I sob through my tears.

Behind me, the car's engine grows louder. Ahead of me, a car turns onto the street. A white car with a track of lights on the hood.

A police car.

"Help!"

Instantly, blue and white lights flash.

Hope blooms.

I think of God's mercy.

And then I'm hit.

My legs snap and for a brief second I'm a rag doll in the air before crashing against a windshield. I see Kameron's horrible twisted and burned face sneer at me through the glass before I flip off the side of the car and land face-first into the street.

A heartbeat later, I see a glorious light.

25

Keisha

A heart-wrenching scream wakes me minutes after I lay my head against the pillow. I'm out of bed in a flash and racing into my children's bedroom in a state of panic. But they're all sitting up in wild-eyed wonderment as well.

Then I hear it again, and I realize the sound is drifting from the floor. Downstairs?

Miz Cleo?

"You guys stay in bed," I say and rush back out of the room. Within seconds, I grab the house key, lock the apartment, and bolt out into the hall. I'm not the only one spilling out of their apartment with curiosity, but when I reach the first landing, I am surprised to see the police at Miz Cleo's door.

Another wail fills the hall, and my eyes dart to the

crumpled figure in the door frame and words literally escape me. What do you say when a superhero has fallen?

Miz Cleo, the strongest and certainly the wisest woman I know, looks like a broken child curled in the doorway. Her head is sunk low and her large hands cover her face while every limb of her trembles like she's havin' an internal earthquake or something. After a quick glance around, I'm not the only one stunned by the sight.

"We're sorry for your loss," one officer says, and they slowly drift away, leavin' the hall and Miz Cleo to her misery.

Only then do I notice the smaller Miz Osceola knelt at her friend's side with a consoling arm draped around her shoulders. I finally unglue my feet from the top of the staircase and fly down the steep stairs to offer some kind of help to a woman who has always looked out for me.

"Help me get her back inside," Miz Osceola instructs, and I obey without question. It's not easy work since Miz Cleo, a heavyset woman, seems to have forgotten how to use her legs or just flat out didn't want to.

People in the hallway start to whisper, and the sound is like a swarm of bees buzzing around us.

Miz Osceola and I grunt and strain, and finally we get Miz Cleo back into her apartment. I give the door a back kick, and I'm grateful the irritating buzzing stops. Still, I wait until we get her to the plastic-covered sofa before I ask, "What happened?"

Suddenly, a baby's cry fills the apartment.

"Oh, Lord, the baby," Miz Cleo moans, snapping out whatever trance that possessed her seconds before. "I gotta see about the baby." She bounds up off the sofa and takes off toward the bedrooms.

I turn my curious gaze back to Miz Osceola's troubled face. "I know it's none of my business," I start.

Miz Osceola flutters a hand to cut me off. "You may as well know. The whole complex is gonna know by mornin'." She exhales a deep breath and shakes her head, but I still have to wait a second or two for an explanation.

"Takiah is dead."

I pull a deep breath myself, but I'm not surprised; it's more of a "Damn."

"We just left her a few hours ago," Osceola says, shaking her head. "Had a beautiful service at the church and . . ." She doesn't finish her sentence.

Our gazes are both locked on the back hallway, waiting for Miz Cleo to reemerge now that the baby's cries have died down.

"Overdose?" I whisper, drawing the only conclusion that makes sense.

Silence and then she whispers, "No."

This time I'm pricked by surprise, and I glance back at Miz Osceola's butter-colored face.

"Police says she was run over by a car."

Now I'm convinced the older lady is talking in a foreign language or, at least, about someone else.

"Witnesses say she was runnin' down the street naked, screaming. They found Pastor Meyer in the church parking lot, stabbed."

"What?" I need to sit down.

"He gave a description before he—"

"No." I shake my head. It's been some years since I've been in church, but I'm aware of Pastor Meyer and his good work in the community: feeding and clothing the homeless, waging war against the drug lords, and fighting to get prayer back in the schools. Sure I've heard wild rumors here and there, especially in my kitchen hair shop, but that was all they were . . . but why was Takiah and Pastor Meyer together? And why was she naked?

I swallow my questions and return home after Miz Cleo piled her best friend and her great-grandbaby into the car and headed down to the hospital to identify Takiah's body.

By morning, Christmas Eve, Takiah and Pastor Meyer's drug abuse and illicit affair is headline news.

"We have to end this."

I've been fearing the day Shakespeare would say those words, and just as I predicted, I'm heartbroken. "Why?"

Shakespeare glances over his shoulder and back at me, tangled in his sheets. "Is that a real question?"

I close my eyes, and take a deep breath, but the tears come all the same. I want to beg and reason with him; however, what reasoning can I use to convince him to keep fucking his brother's wife? Don't worry. Smokey will never know? We've come too far to stop now? I love you?

"I'm sorry, Keesh," he adds pitifully.

Silently, I sit up from the bed and reach for my rumpled clothes pooled on the floor. I gave Smokey the excuse that Shakespeare and I were wrapping a few last-minute Christmas gifts for the children. Of course, Smokey took the lie without question. And why wouldn't he?

I've been his ride-or-die chick since high school, and Shakespeare has always been his brother's keeper. He trusts us.

The poor fool.

I start to get dressed.

"Aren't you going to say something?"

"What would you like for me to say?" I ask, pretending I don't hear the hope in my voice. Is he not sure about ending this? Was I wrong that this was just physical between us?

"I love my brother," he says, as if I doubted it.

"I know." I continue dressing.

Shakespeare doesn't budge from his side of the bed. He just sits there with his head low. You'd think he'd just been handed a death sentence.

"Don't worry," I say, feeling a need to comfort him. "Smokey will never know."

"Does that make it better or worse?"

The misery in his eyes tugs at me. He's definitely taking all of this much harder than I am. For me, my marriage has been over for a long time, and as soon as I finish hair school and get my license, I'm out of Bentley Manor. Come hell or high water.

The fact of the matter is, I can't love Smokey to recovery. His last attempt to get clean lasted all of forty-eight hours. I'm tired of the police showing up at my door and staring at that brunette bitch paramedic while I nurse another black eye or broken rib.

I love Smokey.

But I love myself more.

"When are you going to leave him?" Shakespeare asks, as if reading my thoughts.

I'm silent for a long time and then, "Soon."

The way his body deflates, you would think we were the ones divorcing.

"It'll kill him, you know?"

It's my turn to exhale. "If I stay, it will probably kill me."

In truth, the only time I feel alive is when I'm locked in Shakespeare's arms, each imagining we were getting something other than an orgasm. For me, it was love. Him? I'm still not exactly sure.

I slip on my festive Christmas sweater without bothering with the complications of a bra. I just cram it and my panties in my purse. The faster I can get out of here, the better. When I rush toward the bedroom door, his next words stop me.

"I love you, too."

Finding his words too incredible to believe, I turn around and face him. The way his eyes dart around the floor, I'm positive I didn't hear him right.

"This whole situation is fucked up." He exhales, exploding to his feet and stalking forward. "After what happened to Devani I thought . . ." His shoulders droop even lower. "I don't know what I thought."

"You love me?" I can't get over that part. Hell, I'm not sure I love myself. Not the way I should.

Shakespeare nods before our eyes lock.

"I think you're just feeling . . . lonely. We both are." I can't believe the words flowing from my mouth, but I do recognize the truth. In the space of a heartbeat, he closes the distance between us, and my knees weaken. I want to make love to him again. One last time. Something I'll remember for the rest of my life.

"I wish things were different," he adds, cupping my chin. "I wish you could be mine."

I want to scream that I am his; that nothing has to change. But I can't get myself to say the lie. This is temporary. We are temporary.

"We still have a couple more hours," I whisper, walking my hand up his bare chest. "Tomorrow we can go back to being in-laws."

Sad acceptance twinkles in his eyes. In a flash, my clothes are back on the floor, and our bodies snap together like pieces of an old puzzle. I don't know how he does it, but every inch of me feels loved.

I wish I could explain how it feels to have his cock stroking me, one glorious inch at a time. I love feeling his muscles quiver around and inside of me. And his kisses . . . He kisses me like I'm the most delicious thing he has ever tasted.

God, why does this ever have to end?

Click.

Shakespeare and I freeze.

"Did you hear something?" I ask.

Shakespeare bounces off the bed, and I quickly gather the cotton sheets around my body and follow him out into the dark apartment. I don't know what we heard, but I'm halfway expecting to find my husband in the living room with a nine-gauge ready to blow us to hell for betraying him.

Truth be told, I wouldn't blame him.

But there's no one in the apartment.

"I guess we're just hearing things," Shakespeare says after a thorough search.

I bob my head in agreement, but I can't make myself believe it. Someone was in here.

"I better go," I say, racing back to the room for my clothes. This time, Shakespeare doesn't stop me, even though I can feel he wants to.

Dressed, I walk back into the living room and retrieve my purse and the alibi gifts.

Shakespeare is sitting before the television; a news reporter rehashes the Pastor Meyer story and adds that the police have arrested thirty-two-year-old Kameron Ray, husband to Takiah, for the two deaths.

"Domestic violence," I whisper. "Story of my life."

Shakespeare stands.

"I don't blame you for wanting to leave," he says softly. "But you know he loves you, right?"

My tears gave me no warning, but here they are, streaming down my face while I look up to the man I wished my husband could be. "Yeah. He loves me to death."

"C'mon. You know it's not like that. Smokey would never . . . I mean, he loves you too much to . . ."

I laugh, even though there's not a damn thing funny.

"Keesh—"

"I better go." I sidestep his grasp and walk right past the best thing that ever happened to me.

26

Princess

Bentley Manor.

I don't know why I thought it would look any different or why I thought shit would change.

It seems like more than three months since I left here in handcuffs. I feel like years done been added to my life because of all the shit I been through.

But its time for moving on. Doing better. Being better.

Just before the police cruiser turns through the front gates, I hear one of the lookouts holla a signal to the hood boys. I know once we pull into the parking lot that there won't be a dope dealer, dope user, or anybody on the run from a warrant hanging around. Shit, them fools hit the bricks as soon as they know the police were rolling through the hood.

"Which building?" the young dark-skinned police officer asks.

"Second one on the right."

He pulls right into a spot in front of the building.

When I was locked up I dreamt of the day I would return to Bentley Manor in a stretch limo, dressed from head to toe in Gucci or some shit, with enough diamonds to make the sun look dull while I fanned myself with a wad of hundred dollar bills (big faces). Everybody would be shouting my name. Princess! Princess! Prin—

"Right this way, ma'am."

I come up out of my dream with a quickness and look at the white heavyset female officer waiting to escort me inside. Climbing out the back of a police cruiser wearing a dusty and crusty Waffle House uniform with some ten-dollar black Air Faker 1 sneakers is a helluva way from that dream.

It's cold out, so the usual hoopla of the parking lot is not poppin' off today as I follow the po-po into the building and up the stairs. I am so nervous abut seeing Queen for the first time since that day I flipped out on her ass. I am determined to knuckle up and not show that it bothers me.

The female officer knocks, and I hold my breath as the door to my past opens. Queen is standing there with this look on her face like she ain't in the mood for me, the police, or anything else. *Except some damn man,* I think, hating the disappointment I feel because Queen *know* I been in jail and *doesn't know* if I'm sleeping in the streets. She doesn't care.

The male officer removes his hat. "We called about your daughter asking us to escort her here for her personal items."

"Come on in," Queen says, not even looking at me before she turns and walks to my old bedroom. "I *ain't* gots all day."

The female officer reaches back to squeeze my hand. Just that quick she done pick up on my story with this Queen. I know she feels sorry for me.

Everything about the apartment looks the same to me except for the tall skinny man lying on the fake leather couch flipping through the channels with his shoes off looking comfortable as a bitch. Obviously Cash is out and this one is in. Another one bites the dust. As I walk into my bedroom, I wonder what his problem is. I done figured out my momma has issues and that all the men she fucks with has issues of they own. Like they bullshit-ass lives draws them together or some shit.

I work quick to fill the garbage bags I brought with my clothes from the scratched dressers and tiny closet that ain't big enough for a rat to spin in. I try not to shake when I put my hands inside the lining of that old pleather coat. The envelope holding my half of the prize money and the couple of hundred bucks I made working for Danger is gone. I look over my shoulder at Queen and when she gives me a look like "Prove I took it," I just turn away from her and shove the coat in the bag. I blink away my tears as I grab the two or three pairs of old, curved shoes at the bottom of the closet.

Damn shame. After living on this earth for eighteen years I can fit everything I own in one fucking garbage bag. On top of that the few dollars I earned on my own is gone. I want that money more than these too-small clothes.

I drop the bag to bend over and flip the flimsy top mattress off the box spring.

"Y'all just gone sit by and let her tear up my house?" Queen screams. She steps toward me, but the male officer steps in front of her with his hand on his nightstick.

I reach my hand inside the mattress, and one by one, I pull out my precious journals.

"What the hell is she taking out of there? Those are my property," Queen yells as she twists and turns to the left and right to look past the officer.

"Hey, what's going on in here?"

I look up to see the man off the couch standing in the doorway.

"Lisco Wallace, I think you got enough troubles of your own with your recent arrest for whupping this same woman without you jumping into somebody else's business," the female officer tells him with her hand lightly resting on the gun in her holster. "And we got a call about you threatening an old woman who lives out here 'cause she wouldn't let you smoke dope in her building. You're lucky to be out on bond. Why don't you go on back on that couch and mind your business? Thank you."

He turns his humbled ass right around and walks on out of the room and our business. *So Momma got another woman beater. If she like it, I love it,* I think as I start dropping the journals into the bag atop my clothes.

"Those are mine!" Queen screams again.

"Hold on one sec," the female officer says to me, moving over to take one of the journals out of my hand.

I lock my eyes with Queen as the officer flips through the pages. Her flips become slower as she begins to actually read what I wrote. I see the tears fill the woman's eyes. She hands me the journal as she looks at Queen with angry eyes.

Queen shifts her eyes away from her.

"Those are hers," the woman says with a hard voice. "Her nightmares. Her stories. Her pain. Her words. I ought to arrest your ass for endangering the welfare of your child."

Queen looks like she wants to faint. "What are you talkin' 'bout? I don't know what you're talkin' 'bout!"

She's pathetic.

"She didn't know," I lie. "I never said nothing to her about it."

The officer's face softens as she looks at me. "You should tell her—"

I shake my head. "Ain't nothing to talk about. I just want to leave."

The officer nods, but I don't miss the long look she gives her partner. I follow them out of the room and the apartment.

I nod and pretend to listen as she tells me about counseling and getting help. Maybe one day, but for now I just want out of Bentley Manor and all the hell I been through here.

"Hold on, Princess. Hold on."

We just reached the bottom of the stairwell. I look up at my mother coming down the stairs. She stops on the second level and roughly pushes a wad of money at me. "That's all that's left. I had some bills. Huh, take it," she says.

As soon as I close my fingers around the money she turns and jogs back up the stairs.

The cops look at me as I count the money. Fifty lousy dollars. I know I had close to five hundred dollars stashed away.

I stick the money in my bra. Fuck it. At this point it beat a blank.

As soon as I walk out the building, Miz Osceola walks up to me bundled in her wool coat and cap. She pulls me close to her for a hug.

I smile and let myself enjoy being touched with love.

She fires questions at me fast as she rubs my cold bare hands.

"You got somewhere to stay?"

"When did you get out?"

"Are you in more trouble?"

"You got some way I can call you?"

I hardly had time to answer her before she talks right on.

"That man your momma got now is worse than all the rest," Miz Osceola says with a mournful shake of her head. "That fool threatened to shoot me and Cleo but let him try and he'll meet our friend Louise 1 and Louise 2—our Louisville Sluggers."

I just laugh.

"Baby, I see you're working. That's good. Real good."

I smile at her face filled with lines and wrinkles but sweet as pie. "Yeah, I like it."

"You welcome to stay with me, baby," she offers.

"I'm all right," I tell her, letting myself have one more hug. I think of my granny and hug her a little closer as I smell her neck.

"I'm so sorry how things turned out 'tween you and your momma."

"I heard on the news 'bout Miz Cleo's granddaughter," I say, changing the subject. "Please tell her how sorry I am."

"I will." Her eyes sadden. "She taking it pretty bad but in time she'll be just fine."

"I'm sorry, ladies, but we have to go," the male officer says.

Miz Osceola holds on to my hands with enough strength to surprise my young-buck ass. "It's Christmas tomorrow. You come and spend the day with me if you feeling lonely. I'll pay for the taxi to get you here and back home."

"I would but I have to work tomorrow, Miz Osceola," I tell her. "But I'll come and visit you. Okay?"

"You promise?" she asks as she reaches in her coat pocket and slips me a twenty-dollar bill.

"I promise." I press the twenty back into her hand before I pick up my bag and climb into the backseat of the cruiser.

As it pulls away, I let myself have one last look at Bentley Manor, because I feel like it will be a long time before I see that fucked-up, tore-down motherfucker again.

"Home sweet home." I stand back and look at the small room that is barely bigger than a damn bathroom. It makes Bentley Manor look like a damn mansion or some shit. The thin walls, flat paint, lone twin bed that's as lumpy as a bag of lima beans, and a chair that rocks but ain't a rocking chair.

I use twenty dollars out the money Queen gave back to me to buy a colorful bedspread, lamp, and picture frame from the dollar store. In the frame is a picture of me and Lucky—I sat that on my bed.

I have to share the one bathroom with eight other women—most who just got out jail like me. And living across the street from a liquor store next door to a church is crazy as hell, but for now this room is mine.

And the word "mine" ain't never sound so sweet.

After the last two weeks of rushing from work to try and make it to one of the shelters in time to get a bed, I knew I had to find something a little more permanent. Sometimes I would make it and get a bed. Other times me and forty other women would sit up all night in the lobby of another shelter that was out of beds but didn't have the heart to turn us out onto the street. I hated the nights I had to sleep in the park or buy coffee all night in a doughnut shop so that they would let me sit in one of the booths. Washing my few clothes in a sink if I couldn't afford the Laundromat. Eating nothing but old Waffle House food. Sometimes going days with washing up in the sink and dying for a shower.

I'm thankful for this spot.

Thankful as hell.

27

Woo Woo

I'm going to leave my husband for Hassan.

I will wait until after the holidays and tell him it just isn't working because I like to think I'm not that heartless a bitch. Still, I've made up my mind, and it wasn't easy. But if being with Hassan is equal to being true to me, then it's time for me to step up and be a woman about mine.

It's time for the truth.

Hassan knows that I am ready to come back to Bentley Manor and be with him. We will be together. All I asked for was to give me until after the holidays.

It's sad because my husband doesn't know a thing.

Phipps Plaza is packed with last-minute shoppers as Reggie and I weave our way through the crowds hand in hand. There are many, many good things about my husband, but he is a compulsive procrastinator. Why else would he wait until Christmas Eve to buy his mother a present?

I think he just wants to prove that he doesn't mind that my new microbraids are back in full effect. I compromised on the nails, though. They're back to the full two inches, but I have them painted clear with a white airbush design on the whole nail.

We laugh like old times as he buys his mother a pair of diamond and gold earrings from Ross-Simmons. "I think she will like them," I tell him as I run my hand down his strong lower back.

He looks down at me and smiles. "But you don't, right?"

I start to lie and say of course. I start to deny me and say you're right, but his words ring out to me:

If you feel like you weren't true to yourself then blame yourself, baby . . . not me.

"No, it's not me," I admit.

As the salesgirl moves away from us to wrap the earrings, he reaches into the jacket of his black leather coat. He pulls out a gold cardboard jewelry box. "I think these are more your style," Reggie says as he hands me the box with hesitant eyes. "At least I hope so."

"It's not Christmas," I complain weakly.

"The moment seems right and it's just one of your gifts. Santa has plenty under the tree for you still."

He wants to please me, I think as I reach up to stroke the side of his face before I open the box. I smile as tears I can't even explain fill my eyes. I swallow over a lump in my throat as I pick up the pair of very big, very ghetto, door-knocker bamboo earrings. I laugh as I look at this man. This good and honest man who loves me. Who adores me. Who deserves better than me. Better than my sorry-ass love.

"You like 'em?" Reggie asks as he uses his thumb to wipe a tear from my eye.

"This . . . this is definitely WooWoo," I tell him softly. "Thank you. I love 'em."

Reggie bends down to press his mouth to mine. "I love you just the way you are," he whispers against my lips.

I force a smile.

The salesgirl hands him the receipt and a small gift bag with the package inside. "We better hit the road. Christmas Eve dinner at my mom's is a big deal."

He offers me his hand. I take it. Our fingers entwine. We walk together out of the mall. We are just walking up to Reggie's black Camry when I catch sight of Hassan and his crew walking toward the mall.

Our eyes lock before those green eyes shift down

to take in my hands entwined with my husband's. *Oh God, this bitch better not trip.*

"You're going to love my Aunt Dalia," Reggie is saying as my heart pounds like a drum until it deafens me to the rest of his words.

Hassan's face twists in anger as his steps falter behind his friends. I see their eyes on me. Some snicker. Some wiggle their tongues at me through the letter *V* they make with their fingers. I hear their insults without words being spoken. Dyke. Pussy licker. Dildo lover.

That I don't care about. I'm prepared to handle all that with Hassan at my side. Just not today. Not in front of Reggie. He hasn't done a damn thing but love and accept me. He doesn't deserve this.

Please, Has. Please, I try to beg with my eyes.

Hassan walks past us and I release a breath thinking some crazy-ass scene has been averted. Thank God.

"Man, you know what? Fuck *that*."

I turn at Hassan's words to see his friends walking into the mall as he jogs back behind us. His face is so filled with rage.

"WooWoo, you just gone walk by me and act like we ain't been fucking around for the last two damn years 'cause you with your whack-ass husband."

I'm cheating on my husband. I'm a week from walking into a full-blown lesbian relationship. I'm headed back to living in the hood to be with this nigga and he can't do this for me? I ain't shit for all the bullshit I put Reggie through, but in that moment I am so disappointed in Has that I dislike him.

Reggie turns. I look up. His face is confused as he looks at Hassan and frowns before he looks down at me. "What the fuck is he talking about?"

Okay, Reggie hardly ever curses so this is bad. This is big-time bad.

Shit.

"Tell him, WooWoo. Tell him how you love me. How you want me. Tell him. Tell him you would come to me late at night and beg me to eat your pussy. Tell him how you called me last night from y'all's house and told me you're leaving his ass for me. Tell him."

"If you have something to say to my wife you can say it to me," Reggie says, releasing my hand to take two steps toward Hassan.

"*Your* wife?" Hassan laughs, all sarcastic-like. "Man, fuck your corny ass. You better raise up out of my face."

I stand there, and it's like watching a really bad movie as this woman living life as a man is only five foot seven and stepping to a six-foot man as if she really can beat him. Is Hassan crazy?

Reggie takes his hands and pushes Hassan roughly out his face before he looks over his shoulder at me. "You been cheating on me with this fool?" he asks, his eyes so filled with pain and disbelief and just a bit of hope that this whole thing is not true. "You're leaving me for *this* clown? Is this who you want?"

I look from the woman I love to the man I married. The words won't come. It isn't supposed to go down like this. This isn't the plan. I never wanted to hurt Reggie. I just want to be happy.

"No, you know what? I'm not standing here like a chump while *you* decide what it is you want." Reggie is so angry at me as he turns and stalks away. Suddenly he turns back to look at me as he points his finger accusingly. "You cheated. You disrespected our vows and home and the life we were building. *You* don't get to decide."

I see Hassan run up and rear back to swing on Reggie while he's not looking. "No!" I scream, but it's too late. The blow lands in Reggie's chest and instinctively he swings back, landing a crushing blow to Hassan's jaw that sounds like wood splintering.

I wince and cover my mouth with both my hands. I ache to know that I am the cause of this. I turn to run to Hassan, but Reggie storms past me to snatch him up from the ground by the collar. "No, Reggie, that's a woman," I holler, grabbing his arm.

"What?" he asks as he looks over his shoulder at me, more confused than ever.

"Don't hit her," I yell out to him.

He looks down at Hassan, who is still stunned from the blow. "You have got to be kidding me," he says as he releases Hassan and looks at me again. "You're *gay?*"

Tell him. Tell him. But I can't. I don't want to hurt him. The pain I see in his eyes hurts me deeply. I just want to go to him and hold him close and tell him it's all a lie. Not because I want the marriage—I don't—but because I don't want to hurt him this way.

It *isn't* a lie. It's a truth I wasn't ready to face.

Hassan shakes his head as he jumps to his feet. "Nobody puts their fucking hands on me," he says coldly.

I feel relief flood me. Hassan's okay.

Reggie laughs as he jiggles his keys in his hands.

"What the fuck is so funny?" Hassan yells as his mouth thins until it's almost white.

"You," Reggie fires back. "You just some little confused girl playing dress-up."

"And you some whack-ass Oreo tryin' to be white," Hassan spits back.

This isn't right. Reggie deserves better than this. I can handle Hassan later—we have forever—but for now I just want to get Reggie away from this crazy-ass scene. *He deserves that much respect.*

I run to him and clutch at his chest. "Reggie, let's just go home," I tell him as tears fill my eyes.

"What!" Hassan exclaims behind me.

"You must be crazy," Reggie tells me as he looks down at me and shakes my hands from his body. The look in his eyes makes me feel so cold inside. So lost. So fucked up.

"I just wanna go home, Reggie, please."

Hassan walks up and grabs a fistful of my braids to jerk my head around. "Bitch, you been fucking me around for two years with your wishy-washy shit."

That light in Hassan's eyes scares the shit out of me. That uncontrollable rage that boils deep inside of him is glistening like fire in the green depths.

"I ought to kill your motherfucking ass," he whispers in my face.

"Hassan, please," I whisper back. Why couldn't he just let me handle this my way?

Reggie grabs Hassan by the throat. "I don't beat women but I swear to God you better let her go or I will snap your damn neck!"

Hassan snatches my hair harder. I cry out in sharp pain.

Reggie tightens his hold on Hassan's slender neck.

In one fluid motion that moves slowly, Hassan releases me and then reaches in his coat for his gun and quickly cocks it as he points it at Reggie. Even as my head is pounding, I step to Hassan to reach for the gun.

POW!

It fires. I feel something hot pierce my shoulder.

Someone in the parking lot hollers out at the sound of the gunfire just as I drop to my knees on the ground. My coat sleeve is red from my blood.

He shot me.

I look from my bloody hand to Hassan just as his arm drops to his side with the smoking gun still in his hand. "Hassan, how could you . . ."

My words fade into nothing as I follow his line of vision behind me. Reggie's body is surrounded by a pool of blood. "Oh my God. Oh My God. Ohmigod ohmigod ohmigod," I mumble, like if I say it enough it will make him move. Like it will make him be all right.

"I didn't mean to shoot him . . ." Hassan mumbles behind me.

"Shut up!" I scream as I crawl to Reggie on my knees. I gasp at the gunshot wound in his side. He is lying still. Deathly still. "Ohmigod, ohmigod, ohmigod."

I rush out of my coat and check my arm to find nothing but a deep bloody gash. The bullet must've skimmed my shoulder before it continued on to lodge in Reggie's body.

I feel his blood soaking through my pants as I wrap my hand around his. It's warm and sticky in complete contrast to the coldness of his touch. I reach in my coat pocket for my cell phone. I'm so frantic that it drops into his blood. There's no time to care as I pick it up to dial 911.

I turn and look at Hassan, standing there in shock even as I report the shooting.

"Do you really think he deserves to die?" I ask him with soft words filled with my anger.

The smell of Reggie's blood sends everything in my stomach in reverse. I want to hold him, but I'm scared to move him. I bend over to press my face against his as I drape my coat over his body. "I'm so sorry, Reggie. I swear . . . I swear I'm sorry. Please."

I press kisses to his face.

The sirens echo around us as I lay there in my husband's blood as chills begin to rack his body. Even as the paramedics lift my body from his, I reach for him. I struggle against them to just touch him. Be with him. Near him.

This wasn't supposed to happen.

I catch sight of the police putting Hassan in the backseat of a cruiser. I run to them. "Now what, Hassan?" I ask, my heart breaking. "Why couldn't you let me do this . . . my way?"

Tears glisten his long lashes. "I love you, WooWoo."

My eyes lock with his until the cruiser pulls off and the face that I love is gone from my sight.

I turn in time to see the paramedics pull the sheet up over Reggie's head.

My husband is dead.

My lover is his murderer.

This is all my fault.

28

Princess

I wake up Christmas morning early as hell, and I lay on my thin mattress listening to the rats trying to tear up shit in the walls while I pretend like it ain't a holiday. Trying to pretend like my life is normal. That's the biggest bunch of bullshit ever.

Most eighteen-year-olds are going to school and getting ready for college. I dropped out of school to work full time just to pay the rent so I won't have to share a park bench with a stranger. There ain't a damn thing normal about that.

I grab my newest journal and bite the tip of my pen before I start to write:

> *I'm officially a high school dropout shacking with rats and roaches big enough to actually*

*chitchat with my ass without a soul to spend
Christmas with because my mother is a man-
hungry bitch and my best friend is dead.
Merry fucking Christmas to me.*

When I can't take no more of Mickey and Minnie I
jump up and throw on my Barney sweatsuit and walk
across the street to the liquor store. I probably
shoulda been headed to the church instead, but whateva. I'm in the store reaching for a bottle of water
when I see this head name Lay-Low motioning for
me to be quiet while he pulls on a ski mask and takes
a gun out the waistband of his pants.

I give him a look like *I don't see you and bitch you
don't see me* before I put that water right on back and
get the fuck out that store. I ain't even trying to get
caught up in *that* shit.

I head back to the boardinghouse, pausing just for
a second when I realize how much it looks more like a
haunted house than a home. Fuck it. Right now it is
all I got and beggars can't be choosy. I'm glad the rest
of the boardinghouse is still sleeping as I jog up the
rickety stairs to my room. With nothing else to do, I
start flipping through some earlier entries in my new
journal. It's the first one I've written in since the day
Lucky died. It feels good to write my thoughts, doo-

dles, or play around with poems and song lyrics again. It feels damn good.

Just yesterday I wrote:

> *Miz Osceola invited me to spend Christmas with her. She even offered to pay for me to get there and back home. I lied and said I had to go to work but I'm working the night shift. I have plenty of time to chill with her. I even want to go. I just don't want to see my mother. The best thing for me is to just stay away from Bentley Manor as long as Queen lives there. It's easier to pretend she doesn't exist if I don't see her.*

I close the journal and bite the top of my pen at the sound of the commotion outside. I dash to the window. The wife of the store owner is on the phone and looking up the street. My head turns to see what she sees. I shake my damn head. Lay-Low's pedaling away on a damn bike while the store owner is running behind him, cussing his ass out in Spanish. Lay-Low is dead wrong for that shit.

It's early Christmas morning. Most people are just getting up to open the presents under the tree with their kids or start their Christmas dinner for their families, and his ass out robbing. Where his kids? Where his family?

Shit, who am I to talk?

"*It's Christmas tomorrow. You come and spend the day with me if you feeling lonely . . .*"

"I bet Miz Osceola has a tree, and turkey, and pies," I say aloud to myself as my stomach grumbles. Sure would beat eating another patty melt at work. I can just stay in Miz Oscela's house. I probably won't see Queen. "Hopefully."

I jump up out of bed and grab my uniform before I can change my mind. Okay, just today and only today I'm going back to Bentley Manor, and then after that I will stay away from that place. Everybody deserves some kind of Christmas. Even me.

I miss the 9:15 a.m. bus and have to walk. It's quicker than waiting on a bus during the jacked-up limited holiday schedule. I don't even mind the cold. The walk wouldn't be so bad if the soles of these cheap shoes didn't feel like walking barefoot on concrete. Still, I remind myself to be grateful for those shoes 'cause they are plenty of folks who ain't got none—period.

So I keep on walking. By the time I turn onto the

block leading to Bentley Manor, I'm sweating *every-where*. I know my ass lost a few pounds my skinny butt can't afford to lose.

A few kids are already outside, riding their bikes or skateboards in this biting-ass cold. A couple of heads are out like the walking dead waiting for their pushers to rise so they can celebrate Jesus with gettin' high. Some of them waved at me as I walk straight up the middle of the parking walk to Miz Osceola's building. I don't even cut my eyes toward the building where I used to live.

As soon as I walk in the stairwell, the smell and sounds of Christmas come at me so strong. Food being cooked. Kids loud as hell as they tear through their presents. All of it echoes to me. Mocking me. Reminding me what I don't have. A family. Now, maybe it's my imagination or what I want so deep down in my soul, but as soon as Miz Osceola opens her door, still dressed in her nightclothes, and pulls me into her tight embrace, it feels like Christmas for me. At least a little bit.

"I had fun today, Miz Osceola," I tell her from the window as I watch the kids enjoying their toys out-side.

"I did, too," she calls from her small kitchenette as she fixes me a plate of food stacked high enough that I either have to eat it at work before I go home or wake up in the morning to a shitload of rats and roaches using that motherfucker like a Shoney's buffet.

I didn't admit to her that I live in a shabby-ass boardinghouse 'cause I don't want her to worry. Okay, truth? I don't want her to feel sorry for me. Anyway, it feel good for somebody to give a fuck.

"I know Cleo enjoyed us visiting her and the baby," Miz Osceola says as she waddles out with this huge aluminum contraption that looks more like a damn boulder than a takeaway plate.

"Yeah, I had fun playing with the baby," I tell her as I take the plate. My hands dip a bit from the first feel of the weight of it.

"Come on. I'll walk you out to the front to get the taxi. You don't want to miss it." She opens her front door.

"No, Miz Osceola, I'll be all right," I tell her as I walk to the door. "You can watch me from the window. That way you don't have to walk all the way to the front and back."

"I am tired," she admits.

We hug. We say the right the things: Good-bye. Call me. Take care.

I hate to leave the warmth and comfort of her house, but I do. As I jog down the stairs, I have to remind myself—or fool myself—that my life isn't that bad. I walk out the building and right into someone. I look up into Queen's face. I step back from her.

"Merry Christmas, Princess," she says, her eyes all soft and her voice all nice.

"Merry Christmas," I say, walking past her with my free hand tucked deep into the pocket of a jacket that used to fit two years ago.

"Princess."

I keep walking and ignore her.

"Princess . . . I didn't know," she calls out to me.

I stop and turn to look at her. "That's not good enough."

"You never said anything—"

"Liar," I scream before I turn and walk away.

"Princess—"

"Queen, get your ass upstairs and fix my food!"

I look over my shoulder as Queen looks up at the building. I follow her line of vision to see her new boyfriend in the window yelling down at her.

"I'm coming," she calls to him.

Just once I wish she'd stand up for herself. Stand up for us. "Ma—"

"Now, Queen!"

She looks at me and I see the fear in her eyes. "That's *your* house. It ain't much but it's yours. Miz Osceola says he's on drugs. Why are you letting him order you around and beat on you?" I ask, feeling my anger at her rising again.

"Queen!"

"Princess, I gotta go—"

She turns and hurries into the building without looking back.

I wonder what kind of childhood my mother had where she always has a need, a desire, a want, to put a man first. Before her child. Before herself.

Boom-Boom-Boom!

The ground rattles under my feet from someone's car system. I turn my head to see a silver chromed-out Escalade pull out of a parking spot to pass me as they head out of Bentley Manor. My eyes fall right on the license plate. DANGER1.

Boom-Boom-Boom!

Danger. Oh shit. Danger? I forgot he has a kid living in Bentley Manor. Fuck it. I have to see if it's him. I have to. *Fuck* that.

"Danger," I call at the top of my lungs as I put those cheap-ass Air Faker 1s to the test and run behind that SUV.

Boom-Boom-Boom!

How will he hear me over the fucking music?

"Danger," I call and call as my heart races and my throat feels dry.

The Escalade slows.

"Danger . . . Danger!" I yell as I near that mother-fucker.

It makes the right turn out the front gate.

Boom-Boom-Boom!

My chest is hurting like crazy. I don't even remember exactly when I dropped that plate. I feel like I'm going to fall the hell out, but something tells me not to stop. Don't give up.

He stops at the gate, awaiting oncoming traffic.

Boom-Boom-Boom!

I just reach the back of the SUV and bang on the rear window like I can afford to pay for that bitch if it breaks. When he turns right and speeds up the street, I collapse right there on the grimy, glass-scattered blacktop. I don't give a shit what the hell I'm lying in as I roll over onto my back. My chest is heaving as I gulp for air.

I ball up my fists and hit the ground in frustration.

Last week on my day off I walked—*walked*—to that old beat-up studio Danger rented to do Q's demo. I walked for two hours, hoping by a stroke of luck he was there or at least the owners knew how I could reach him. When I finally got there and saw it was closed for business, I knuckled up and said it wasn't meant to be, even though my disappointment was so thick I could eat it with a spoon.

Today I just can't even front and fool myself into a damn thing. I want out of the hood. I want a better life.

When the fuck am I finally going to get a break?

Boom-Boom-Boom!

Okay, I know I shouldn't feel so damn sorry for myself, but damn, I was corn-fed on this shit. It's all I know.

Boom-Boom-Boom!.

Okay, maybe it wasn't even Danger. I might have been hollering behind someone I don't even know. And who says Danger still wants to work with me. Produce me. Make me famous.

Not catching up with that Escalade doesn't seem like a big damn deal but *right* now . . . right now it's way more than I can take.

The ground rumbles beneath me.

I look up to see the SUV pull back through the gate. I jump to my feet just as it stops and the tinted driver's-side window lowers.

"What's up, stranger?" Danger calls out to me with his grille damn near blinding me.

I try to play it cool like my ass was not just laid out on the cold-ass ground as I stroll up to the car like *I'm* the baller.

"Nothing. Just enjoying the holidays," I say all cool and calm.

"Yeah, I just dropped my son his Christmas gifts."

"Yeah, I was just headed to work," I tell him, 'bout sick of the chitchat.

His eyes take in my uniform, da-dun-da-duh (i.e., no-name) sneakers, and beat-down ponytail. "I've been trying to reach you. Heard you had to do a little time?"

I swipe the glass chips off my ass. "A little something."

"Well, I'm glad we ran into each other." Danger lifts up in his seat to reach into his back pocket.

He hands me a card. Our hands touch, and the familiar warmth he used to cause in me feels nice. I look down at the card.

"Danger Entertainment," I read aloud before I look up at him, as the butterflies in my stomach start to flutter like crazy.

"Q actually got signed a few weeks ago and I'm working on his debut album," he boasts as he leans his bony elbows out the window.

The diamonds in his watch probably cost enough for me to pay my rent for ten years.

"Congratulations—"

"I ain't forgot what I told you and I can see it all on your face that you ain't forgot either," he teases.

"So what this mean?" I cock my head to the side to look at him with a soft smile that is kinda flirty. Me, flirty?

"You know whassup," he tells me as he reaches out to tap the card. "You ain't do all that running for nothing."

"You saw me, huh?" I feel excited and happy. I ain't got time to worry 'bout being shamed 'bout runnin' like a runaway slave.

"Why you think I turned around?" Danger takes off his baseball cap and puts it back on like he is adjusting the feel of it. "The record execs liked your voice on Q's single. They want to hear something from you. We got to get your style together, Shorty. No offense."

Hell, I feel offended—but whateva.

"I need to get you in the studio for your own demo. You ready?"

I force myself to breathe and not act silly. I force myself to breathe and not cry. Finally. Finally I'm getting a chance. Something good is happening for me. Finally. "Trust I'm *more* than ready," I tell him with the most confidence I have ever felt in my life.

"Look, I got to jet or Sade girl will be trippin'—"

In that moment I don't even care that he's still with her.

"You want a ride to work?"

"Hell, yeah," I say before I walk around the SUV to jump inside.

Leather seats. Wood grain. BOSE stereo system. "This a nice-ass ride," I tell him as he turns around in the parking lot and heads back out through the gate.

"Soon you'll be riding like this all the time. I promise you, Princess."

I smile as I look at him and hold on to the card like it's my lifesaver.

I believe him.

29

Keisha

We may not have much, but my kids still love Christmas. And this time, unlike last year, our plastic Wal-Mart pre-lit Christmas tree that me and the kids spent hours decorating is still standing in the corner of the living room when we all wake up. I wish I could say the same for the Christmas gifts.

"Momma." Jasmine tugs at the pants of my pajamas. "Did Daddy pawn our Christmas gifts?"

Of course he did—or at least he thinks he did. I smile and shake my head.

My children's puzzled faces follow me to the front door, and I'm giddy as a schoolgirl as I race down the hall to Hawkina's place. Like I've said before: Smokey is nothing if not predictable. A few minutes later, the children exploded with cheer when me, Hawkina, and her husband returned to the apartment with the kids' real Christmas gifts.

"Thanks, girl," I tell Hawkina and promise her the next wash and set is on the house.

The kids waste no time tearing into their gifts while I retrieve a disposable camera I picked up last night. No, none of the gifts are fancy, and most all of them come from the Dollar General, but the kids squeal and jump all the same.

None of us miss Smokey.

No one even mentions him.

If the beatings and the affair isn't enough to tell me my marriage is over, this picture-perfect Christmas morning *without* my husband finally makes my heart accept it.

Hours roll by and I allow the children to gorge on everything from syrupy pancakes to cookies to a tree-ful of candy canes. Any guilt I feel is erased with the excuse "It's Christmas."

Uncle Shakespeare showed up shortly before noon. After embracin' the kids and handing them his gifts, we fall into an awkward embrace, wishing each other a Merry Christmas.

It's hard for me to pry myself from his strong arms and his woodsy fragrance. I'm not even gonna front. It's even more difficult not to remember how good he feels when he's inside of me. Shakespeare was the best lover I've ever had—not that there's a long list.

When I successfully move away from his embrace, I glimpse longing in his eyes. Stunned, I shake my head and almost laugh aloud, certain I'm imaginin' things. Let's keep it real—Shakespeare can have his pick of women. I'm only expandin' my heartache, fantasizin' that he has truly fallen in love with a frumpy ex-junkie with four kids . . . who is married to his brother.

I keep forgetting that part.

"I got something for you, too," Shakespeare says, handin' over a small red box with a tiny white bow. "It's just a little something." He shrugs.

I blink and wince almost at the same time. It's not that I didn't think to buy him a gift. I did, but my money is always funny and the General Dollar was all I could afford for the kids.

"I don't . . . I can't . . ."

"Don't worry," he says, readin' my thoughts. "You've given me plenty."

"I can say the same thing about you, puttin' me through school and all," I say, refusin' to take the box.

"I'm not doin' anything I don't want to do." He steps closer to me. "I'm not doin' anything you don't deserve."

My tears are instant, but I resist a trip back into his arms because of the children. Instead, I accept the gift from his large hands, but give him my back while I mop my face. Once that's through, I open my gift with tremblin' fingers. Inside is a small seven-inch glass bottle with sand, tiny seashells, a paper beach umbrella, and if I'm not mistaken, a piece of paper rolled inside.

"What's this?" I ask.

Shakespeare closes the space between us, and I'm once again surrounded by his masculine scent. "It's a message in a bottle. Go ahead. Read the message."

Touched by the unique gift, my tears return, which only makes it harder to uncork the bottle. Seein' I need help, Shakespeare takes over, opens the bottle, and fishes out the small rolled-up piece of paper. The first thing I notice is the message isn't addressed—and it's not signed. It just reads:

You entered my heart at the right time. Healed what needed to be healed and loved what needed to be loved. For that, in my heart, you will always stay.

I smile and will my tears to remain hidden as I look up. "Thanks. You know I . . ." I swallow the words I was about to say and cover with, "I care a great deal for you."

Jasmine pops up between us and tugs her uncle over to their new pile of plastic toys.

An hour before my sister arrives to take me and the kids over to her place for Christmas dinner, I finally start wondering about Smokey's whereabouts.

"Can we go outside and play until Aunt Cheryl comes?" Jackson asks.

I'm torn because I know when my kids step outside, Dollar General will be poked fun of next to the top-of-the-line Wal-Mart and Target gifts. I know it's not supposed to matter, but it does.

"Momma?" Jackson tugs on my legs again.

"Sure, baby. Go on outside."

My four babies jump up and cheer, and then file out of the house to show what Santa brought them.

"What's the matter?" Shakespeare asks, pickin' up on my anxiety.

"Nothing," I lie. The thing is . . . something *is* wrong. I just can't put my finger on it.

"Where's Smokey?" Shakespeare asks for the first time.

"No clue. He jumped out of here with the fake gifts this morning and I haven't seen him since." That wasn't quite right. Smokey wasn't home when I returned last night, but the kids had been tucked into bed. "Who knows where he is," I finally say, but my uneasiness refuses to go away.

"Maybe we should call the precinct." Shakespeare flips open his cell phone and punches one number because he has the po-po on speed dial. How sad is that?

I give Shakespeare's call a half ear while I peek through my dust-covered venetian blinds to see if I can spot my husband shakin' and hustlin' for a hit. Amazingly, the only thing I see is children playin' out in the *U* with their new Christmas gifts.

This is a real Kodak moment: druggies and thieves take a holiday.

Behind me, Shakespeare snaps his phone closed. "He's not there."

"Something's wrong," I say, feeling it for the first time in my bones.

"We don't know that," Shakespeare says. I don't realize that he's walked up behind me until he places a kiss against the back of my head. Then it's all I can do not to melt back into his arms and finish where we left off last night.

Click.

I jumped, the same way I'd jumped last night. This time when I turn toward the door, my husband is standing there with a half-crooked grin and wearing a Santa Claus suit.

"There you are," Shakespeare says, trying to sound relieved, but I catch, and I'm sure Smokey does, too, a nervous titter in his younger brother's voice.

I ease away from Shakespeare, carving a smile on my wooden face. "Where have you been?"

Smokey's black eyes are glossy, but dead.

"I see you scored a hit." I shake my head in disappointment. Same shit. Christmas Day.

"I scored a couple of hits," Smokey brags, his voice thick and slow like molasses.

"Samuel," Shakespeare says, using my husband's real name. "You need to get yourself cleaned up. You promised."

"Shit. I don't see why I got to be the only one keeping promises around here." His emotionless black orbs shift from me to Shakespeare, and it clicks inside my head.

He knows.

That's when I see the gun, clutched at his side.

"What are you doing with that?" Shakespeare asks with a calm I don't share.

Smokey doesn't answer. His hard gaze whips about the room like a second weapon. In my mind, all I can think about is the news report on Takiah. Run down in the street by her husband. Now, less than forty-eight hours later, it's my turn.

"You two have been awfully chummy lately," Smokey finally says. "Someone could get the wrong impression on just who is married to who."

We don't answer, and Smokey's sinister smile dims. "I'm a fuckup. Everyone knows that." He uses the barrel of the gun to scratch his right temple. When he speaks again, it's not clear whether he's talking to us or to himself. "I've tried to kick this shit. God knows I have," he says, shaking his head. "But this shit got me fucked up. I think about it. I dream about crack. It's my mistress, my lover . . . my wife."

My eyes drop to the floor. At the same time, I feel his deadly gaze roam over me.

"But there's not enough room in my life for two wives. Is there, Keisha?"

The tiny apartment suddenly feels like a sauna in the middle of winter. I'm afraid to answer, frightened that my answer would get me a bullet through the head. It wouldn't be the first time. Not here in Bentley Manor.

"Samuel, why don't you put the gun down and we'll talk about this like civil adults?"

In a flash, Smokey aims the gun and squeezes the

trigger. I scream at the sudden blast and the instant shatter of glass from the front window. I glance over my shoulder to see a stunned Shakespeare, sweating and staring at his older brother.

The building is suddenly alive with activity.

"How could you fuckin' do this to me?" Smokey asks through his clenched teeth. "What was the game plan—push me aside and you just step in and take my family?"

"No, Smokey, you got it all wrong."

"Do I?" Smokey laughs. "Then that wasn't you I saw fuckin' my wife last night at your house?"

Click.

The sound outside Shakespeare's bedroom replays in my head, confirming my fate.

"What the fuck is going on over there?" A man's voice booms in the hallway.

Smokey responds by shooting blindly toward the door. "Mind your own fuckin' business!"

I jump back and slam into Shakespeare's broad chest. His arms wrap around me and, to my surprise, I still find comfort within them.

Smokey watches the intimate gesture with a new snarl of disgust. "I bet you two creepin' motherfuckers thought I'd never find out. I might be high all the time, but I ain't blind." Smokey's eyes center on me.

"I've seen how you look at my brother lately. You used to look at me that way. Remember? Back in school? Hmm?"

I swallow the large lump in the center of my throat. "High school was a long time ago," I finally say.

"What? You don't love a nigga no more?"

Hot tears race down my cheeks as I struggle to answer the question. In the end I simply can't. This shit is my fault. I'd given up on him.

"You did this shit to me, Keisha," he whines. "You got me hooked on this shit and now *I'm* the asshole?"

"Samuel, you can't blame—"

Bang!

He shoots down at the floor.

"Shut up!" Smokey roars. "What happened to all that 'my brother's keeper' crap you fed me?"

Shakespeare falls silent, and his arm loosens around my waist.

"Is this how you look after me? You fuck my wife?"

When he doesn't receive an answer, he fires another shot into the floor.

Bang!

My thoughts fly to Miz Cleo and her precious great-grandbaby downstairs.

Chaos continues outside the door.

In the distance, I hear sirens.

The police. Thank God.

Smokey smiles as he looks at me. "What? You think they gonna save your cheatin' ass?" He laughs. "Not this time."

30

Miz Cleo

The world feels like it's been turned upside down. I killed my grandbaby. I may not have been behind the wheel or the one that filled her veins with all that poison, but I led her to Pastor Meyer. I handed her over like a sacrificial lamb and my hands are red from her blood. Osceola keeps telling me I need to pull myself together, but how can I?

She doesn't understand. She has never had children, let alone grandchildren. So how can she truly understand what I'm going through? My faith is shaken and I'm tryna see God in all of this, but I can't.

Takiah came to me for help, and I let her down. Just as I let my own children down. The ones in jail and the ones only God knows where they are. The only one who's been able to put a smile on my face the last two days is my great-grandbaby, Tanana.

As sweet as she is, I wonder whether I'm the best thing for her. Let's face it: I don't exactly have a successful record when it comes to raisin' kids. And I'm old. Because of a host of medical issues, my chances of seeing this child to her own high school graduation is slim. *If* she stays in school.

I got to be honest with you. My spirits are low, and right now it doesn't feel like they will ever rise again.

Bang!

Good Lord, they out there shootin' again. I jump up and race to the phone. It's a shame, but I call the police about as often as I call Osceola. I'm surprised they don't recognize my voice when I call.

"Send somebody over here. They shootin'," I say when the 911 operator comes on the line.

"Where are they shooting, ma'am?"

"Where they always shootin'. At Bentley Manor."

A picture frame next to me explodes. "Oh, hell. They shooting in my place." I drop the phone. And I race to the back bedroom for Tanana. I think I just need to grab the baby and run outside, but then I hear another shot, and that one seemed like it was outside. Suddenly, I'm frozen and don't know what to do, and no place seem safe.

Remarkably, when I glance down into the baby's bed, Tanana is sleeping like she doesn't have a care in the world. The shootin' stops, and I think it might all be over with.

A few minutes later, I hear the police sirens.

"Thank God in heaven," I whisper. Soon it will all be over. Somehow, I manage to relax and grab the empty baby bottle lying next to my great-grand.

I see the blue and white lights flash through the windows and know enough to stay away from them until the trouble has died down.

"I guess I'll go wash this bottle out," I tell myself, but in truth I was already on my way to press my ear to the door and see if I can catch what's going on in the hallway like I usually do.

But no sooner do I step into my living room does my front door bang open.

"What the hell—?"

"Drop your weapon," a man booms.

I'm confused because all I have is a baby bottle.

I stretch the bottle toward him. "I don't have—"

It's all I'm able to say before the bastard shoots me.

31

Keisha

Shakespeare, Smokey, and I jump when we hear the sudden and rapid gunfire below us. None of us say anything, but our eyes all race to the door, wondering what's happening.

"Samuel, put the gun down," Shakespeare urges. "This has gone on far enough."

"Oh, Lawd," someone cries. "You got the wrong apartment! You done shot Miz Cleo!"

My eyes skitter back to my husband. The meaning of it all sinks in, and my eyes well up with tears. "I didn't mean to hurt you, baby."

"Neither one of us did," Shakespeare amends.

"Then why . . . ?" Smokey backhands his tears. "I was trying," he sobs. "I swear to God, I was trying."

"I know you were." I try to push Shakespeare's arm from my waist, but his grip tightens. "Let me go," I tell him and then walk slowly toward my husband-slash-child. "I'm sorry, baby. I was lonely and tired. Do you even remember the last time you've taken me in your arms and even said that you love me?"

His glassy eyes fall to the floor.

"I'm a woman, Smokey," I say, thrusting a finger against my chest. "I'm a woman with needs. All you want and need is your damn crack."

"It's not my fault. I can't get off. *You* got me hooked on this shit."

"*And* I tried to get you off," I shout. I'm no longer willing to shoulder the blame for his addiction. "I got off."

The chaos in the hallway grows to a crescendo, and I hear a small army rush up the stairs.

"It's that apartment down there," someone shouts.

"I'm not as strong as you are," Smokey says, collapsing to the floor, his grip still tight on the gun. "I wish I was."

"You *are*," I assure him and slide down next to him. "You can go back to rehab."

Smokey laughs.

"I mean it," I say. "You can do it this time."

He shakes his head.

A fist pounds on the door. "Open up. Police."

Shakespeare looks over at us, wide-eyed. "Samuel, put down the gun."

Smokey shakes his head. His dead eyes now seem like an endless pool of misery. "I can't," he whines. "It's too hard."

"I know, baby." I try to gather him in my arms, but he pushes me away. "Get the fuck off of me."

I leap back from his sudden burst of anger, and I watch as he waves the gun around. "You don't understand," he sobs. "I don't . . . I can't live without it."

"Open up," the police thunders again.

"I've tried and I've tried and . . ." He looks up at me. "I'm sorry I hit you . . . and I'm sorry you've been so lonely."

His heartfelt words tear my heart in two. Suddenly I remember the teenage boy I fell in love with, the handsome captain of the basketball team that gave me four beautiful babies.

"Last time. Open up!"

"Hold on," Shakespeare shouts to the door and then turns his pleading eyes toward his brother. "Smokey, please."

Tears splash down my husband's face as he

meets his brother's gaze. "You were never my keeper."

"Samuel . . ."

Before I knew it, before I could react, Smokey shoves the gun into his mouth.

"No!"

He pulls the trigger and soaks me in his blood.

Miz Osceola

One Year Later

"Thank you, God, for allowing me to wake up and see another day." I say that every morning as soon as I get up out of my bed and press my feet to the floor.

Ever since last Christmas, I make sure to get up every morning and give The Big One above his due. I'm getting older, and it's time I secure my ties to heaven just a bit. Besides, I'm used to the foolishness that goes on around this place, but a year ago it hit too close to home.

Cleo. My friend. My gossip buddy. My partner in crime. My girlfriend—as the young ones says these days.

I sniff back my tears. It still hurts me so bad to think

of that day. "Whoo," I say as I grab my Bible and read the twenty-first Psalm.

I feel a lot closer to God these days, and that ain't easy to say considering that false prophet, snake in the grass, wolf in sheep's clothing Pastor Meyer.

Humph. *I always knew that granddaughter of Cleo had nothing but heartache written all over her for my friend. The news long moved on to other scandalous stories than Takiah and that undercover crackhead Pastor Myers, but her death is still the talk 'round here. Sleeping and getting high with her grandmother's pastor and then getting run over butt naked in the street by her husband/pusher/pimp ain't easily forgotten.* The Young and the Restless—*move over, here's the real drama. I ain't gone say she got what she deserved or nothing harsh like that, but if you live by the sword, you die by the sword. Point blank.*

I let out a breath as I pull back my curtain and look out at the parking lot below. There's a few of them lost souls up and waiting for the first sign of a dealer to get 'em their fix. God knows how much tail they done sold or things they done stole and pawn to get the money. I shake my head at Delia out there in that cold, shivering in a thin coat, probably don't know or care where her kids are.

I see their heads suddenly perk up before they move

toward the front building. I never deny being nosy, so I move to the other end of the window to see them circled around somebody in an oversized winter coat. "Marcus," I whisper against the frosted window glass when I catch sight of his face.

No matter how much we call the police and local politicians just to stir up enough heat to burn these dealers, you got ten more waiting to make that fast money. And they're getting more violent and mean. More hateful. I ain't surprised at all when Marcus swings on Delia. He 'bout one of the meanest I ever seen. Big whoo power trippin' over sick people addicted to drugs. That make him feel like a man?

He reminds me of that Hassan . . . Leslie . . . whateva. God knows she had so much anger in her, just waiting to be tripped on over nothing. Maybe it had to do with why she dressed up and lived like a man. If she gay she gay, but why the pretending to be a man? That I don't understand. She hung out with men. Talked like a man. And considering that big old black thing she flung at WooWoo, that day they fought look like she pretend to have sex like a man, too. Now that was a mess.

Maybe if she got help for that anger, she wouldn't be sitting in prison with a life sentence for murder.

Couldn't be easy for WooWoo, seeing as how she caused some of that with all her sneaking 'round here and cheating on her husband. Playing two people against each other is like playing with fire. Now she ain't got neither one. Don't know if she decided to be gay or straight. Don't know how come she didn't know what she wanted from the get-go. Sounds like she's just plain selfish to me. She ain't been back to Bentley Manor since. Can't say I know that much about her at all. Heard she live with her sister, but that's as far as the gossip went. Wherever she is, I hope she got her act together.

I groan as I make my way into the bathroom to freshen up for the day. I look at my face in the mirror. A year goes by, and there are a few more wrinkles and a few more pounds and a lot more wisdom. I touch my hair, thinking I can do with a black rinse and press a curl.

Now that Keisha's gone, I'm gone have to find me a hairdresser to wash this gray right out of my hair. I would go to her new big-time, saddity shop, but it will take me two buses and too much time to get to her. She own her own shop, and now I hear she handle famous people hair. Umph, umph, umph. What a difference a year makes. I'm proud of her. Smokey finally freed her with his death. It ain't nice to say but it's the truth. Her and them kids of hers doing better than ever in their new place. Smokey freed his brother, too.

I leave the bathroom and walk into the bedroom to

pick up the book on my night table. "My Brother's Keeper by national bestselling author Shakespeare Williamson," I read out loud. At least all that heartache and hassle his brother put him through was good for something.

I put the book back. I ain't much of a reader, but it feels good to know a big-time writer. I keep it there like a reminder to what good can come up outta this hellhole. It ain't where you're from, its where you're going.

I throw on a Bash Bush T-shirt and a pair of jeans before I head out my bedroom as fast as I can. My little apartment get mighty hot when I got the oven on, and today I plan to throw down with another big old Christmas feast. Ain't got no family of my own, so it's more habit than anything. I always wind up giving the food away. I just think a home should smell like some good old soul food on the holidays.

And if I didn't get that bird into the oven, then it'll be next Christmas before it's done. I turn on the TV in the living room before I make my way into the kitchen. Just like my own rhythm, it don't take long at all before I got them pots rolling and my bird baking. I'm wiping my hands on a dish towel when I look up at the TV and see Princess's video.

"And don't she look pretty," I say as I stand there and

watch her all did up with makeup and fancy clothes. It ain't my first time seeing the video, but I watch it again and again like it's the first time. I hate that she ain't never been back to Bentley Manor, but ain't nothing here for her. Her silly momma still got men moving in and out that apartment like roaches. Got the nerve to be 'round here bragging on her daughter. Humph, bet she don't like that her daughter don't fool up with her ass at all. No, that girl off living her dreams. Her single "It's My Time" is the number one R&B record in the country. Now that's how you make a fool like Queen regret neglecting her child. I chuckle and boogie a little as I watch Princess dancing with a bunch of boys behind her. She look good too. Real good. She got the right title for her song, 'cause it sure look like it is her time.

My doorbell sounds off, and I keep my eye on the TV as I boogie these old bones on to the front door. "I'm doing things by my own design . . . You better act right, get straight . . . It's my time," I sing along with her as I open the door.

"Merry Christmas, you old fool."

I smile big and wide as I eye Cleo standing there holding Tanana's hand. I want to get all mushy and hug her up, because I know this time last year she could have died. But that old bird is like a Timex, because she took a lickin' and kept on tickin'. She walks with a little limp, but she made it through. She's here and that's all that matters. Thank God. We old, but ain't neither one of us ready to meet Him just yet.

Hell, we still got plenty to see and to tell.

Acknowledgments

From Meesha

Just a quick thank you to:

God—4 everything, 4 ever, 4 always.

Tony—for the last ten years.

Letha (My Moms), Caleb (My Big Brother), and the rest of my huge family—for your love.

Claudia Menza of the Menza Baron Agency—for your wisdom, your knowledge, and your calm.

Meghan Stevenson and the rest of the fabulous Simon & Schuster/Touchstone family—for your professionalism and expertise.

De'nesha Diamond—for your hard work and great words.

Morrison Creative Trends in South Carolina—for keeping me looking lovely.

Kim Louise—for your friendship.

To anyone I forgot—for knowing to blame my head and not my heart.

Peace & Blessings,

Meesha

From De'nesha

Lord Almighty—thanks for inspiring me to write Takiah's story—to remind people that it's never too late. To Granny, for being the best guardian angel—ever.

To my sister Channon "Chocolate Drop" Kennedy—you're the best.

To my other sister, Charla "McNugget" Byrd—you do you, ma.

To my beautiful niece, Courtney, I can't wait until we get out the Dora phase.

To Kathy Alba, thanks for being my best friend for twenty-odd years and always coming through in a pinch. To Charles Alba—thanks for taking care of my girl—and hell no, I STILL ain't paying you two dollars.

To the ByrdWatchers fan club—you always been so loyal and thanks for encouraging me to do what I do. To Angie Clark—a very strong black woman, doin' her thang.

To the Barretts—my second family. I love you all very much.

To my favorite cousin: Josphine Johnson—I appreciate you and your talks about the facts of life.

A big, big thank-you to Deidre Knight of the

Knight Agency for sticking with me for the past ten years. The minute you heard about this idea you were all over it. I love you for that. To Meghan Stevenson at Touchstone, for keepin' the party rollin'.

And to Meesha aka Niobia—much love for your talent. Let's see if we can do it again.

Best of love,

De'nesha

MEESHA MINK is the pseudonym for Niobia Bryant, a national bestselling and award-winning author with over ten works of fiction. Currently she writes sexy urban fiction for Simon & Schuster/Touchstone, drama-filled women's fiction for Kensington/Dafina Trade, and "sexy, funny, and oh so real" romance for Kensington/Dafina Romance. The author splits her time between her hometown of Newark, New Jersey, and her second home in South Carolina. For more on Meesha, visit: www.myspace.com/meeshamink and for more on the author's works under her real name, visit: www.niobiabryant.com.

DE'NESHA DIAMOND is the pseudonym for Adrianne Byrd, a national bestselling author of thirty multicultural romances. Adrianne Byrd has always preferred to live within the realms of her imagination, where all the men are gorgeous and the women are worth whatever trouble they manage to get into. As an army brat, she traveled throughout Europe and learned to appreciate and value different cultures. Now she calls

Georgia home. For more information on De'nesha Diamond and Adrianne Byrd's work, visit: www.adriannebyrd.com

Both authors can be reached at the official HOOD-WIVES website: www.hoodwives.com

For a sneak peek into the hard days, steamy nights, and the *men* of Bentley Manor, just turn the page.

Cuz a player, a pimp, a dealer, and a killer hustle for their lives in . . .

The Hood Life

Coming from Touchstone Books in January 2009

Miz Cleo

I've seen a lot in my seventy-three years. But heartache is nothing new in Bentley Manor. In fact it comes with the territory. But we all do the best we can. Take things one day at a time.

Now that I'm raising my great-grandbaby, I fall on my knees every night, praying she'll be the one to escape the family curse of poverty. I pray the Lord will guide her away from all the pimps, playas, dealers, and killers roaming this place we call home.

Most travel down the same self-destructive path, ignoring the bodies that fall by the wayside and dragging these women down along with them.

I suspect I'll be praying for the rest of my days.

Pimp

Pussy is big business.

And I'm a businessman—a damn good one. Yeah, I dibble and dabble in a few other things. Who doesn't? If a nigga wants to carve himself a piece of the American pie, he's got to get his hustle on. You feel me? I'm sure you do. Tavon Johnson is the name and pussy is my game.

'Course, on the streets, they call me Sweet Diamondtrim Johnson. Diamonds are my trademark. So much so that my girls keeps their pussies shaved and sport diamond tattoos inches above their clits.

If you're wondering how I got into this business, I guess you could say I sort of fell into it. I popped my first cherry at twelve. Her name was Renee Collins. I swear to this day that she has the sweetest piece of pussy a nigga ever tasted. And 'course I bragged this shit to my best friend, Destin. Bragged so much that he promised to give me his allowance for a full month if I let him have a go at Renee himself.

Renee was pissed, but it had been easy to convince her fuckin' Destin was her chance to prove how much she loved me. I gotta tell ya: watching her in action with my best friend was an incredible high. Watching her do a few more boys behind the schoolyard and under the gym bleachers convinced me that I really did love her.

All in all, it was just another reason in a long list of why I married her. For the record, she still has the sweetest pussy I've ever tasted.

So what's your fantasy? I have every kind of ho you can imagine: black, white, Puerto Rican, or Asian. You name it, I got it. You want a streetwalker, a glamorous escort, a porno star, or maybe you're one of those down-low brothers. Don't matter. I got a few dicks on the payroll, too. It's all pussy to me.

Being in the biz for a quarter, I've seen it all. You can whip them, tie them up, and you can even piss on them, if that's your thing. It's all negotiable. But don't get it twisted, pimpin' ain't easy.

Playa

Life is so fucking good . . . *especially* for a fine motherfucker like me. Just twenty-eight, high yellow, gray eyes, good hair, toned body, and a big dick—oh, I'm *the* shit and I know it. I've always known it and there ain't shit in this world I want that I can't get, especially if what I want belongs to a woman. Money. Clothes. Jewelry. Three hots and a cot. And for sure pussy. Pussy. And more pussy.

Wasn't too many men that can twist a woman's legs like a pretzel and then lay that pipe so good that she forget how I had her positioned.

When I say jump, my bitches ask, "How high?"

When I say suck this dick, they ask, "How deep?"

When I say give me money, their *only* question better be, "How much?"

I roll out of the bed and reach for my brown Dickies pants from the floor.

"here you going, Rhak?"

ease a heavy breath as I dress before I turn to
ok down at her. Not that looking in her face or calling
her by her name matters worth a damn. To me all these
bitches is one and the same. No matter how much they
suck and fuck me, ain't none of these tricks mean more
to me than the other. Not even my girl, Shaterica.

"I'm heading back to the crib, baby," I tell her in my
smoothest voice. (I call them all "baby" to keep from saying the wrong name at the wrong damn time.)

Taira flips the covers back, revealing her brickhouse
body covered by the tightest, smoothest, and darkest
skin ever. *Humph*. Her pussy is just as tight.

"I gotta go, but I'll get up with you tomorrow," I tell
her with "the look"—deep stare, hard jaw, head tilted
slightly to the side with a wink followed by half a smile. It
gets them every time. I will be eternally grateful to my
Uncle LeRon for teaching me that and some more shit that
keeps this true playa for real in true pussy forever.

Like clockwork, "the look" turns her frown up the
fuck side down. Shit, don't hate the player . . .

I leave her bedroom and ignore the hell out her
snot-nose kids sitting in the living room as I stroll out
the house, forgetting her with as much ease as I please.
I done got what I want from her ass. My dick done
got good and wet and my pockets are a little fatter. I
finger the crisp hundred-dollar bill she gave me. *She
thinks* of it as a loan and *I know* it's payment for services rendered. Translation: She might as well kiss this
bill good-bye. Besides, my girl been nagging me to pay
half on the car note, so now I can get her ass off my
back.

I'm singing along with the radio as I drive up Piedmont in my black Honda Accord—well, it's Shaterica's, but fuck it, what's hers is mine. All she ever does is hand me the keys with a smile and I'm out of Bentley Manor. I drive it, fuck in it, pull new bitches in it, and do what the hell I please in it. Just last week I drove over to this little white chick I fuck with over in Buckhead. I slipped and spent the night with that bitch and my girl was mad as hell and straight mean-mugging me when I finally walked through the door the next morning. I shot her a lie about getting drunk and falling asleep on one of my homeboys' couch—picture that shit really happening; shit, I ain't one of them cruddy down-low brothers. My name is Rhakwon, not Junior.

Not that I don't care about my lady. She real good to me and I know it. Even though she say I don't recognize all the shit she does for me, but that's *her* job to be good to me. She knew that when she filled out the application and whenever her ass feel like she can't keep up the job description of being my girl, then I'll fire her. She know what's up.

The Killer

For ten years I've been rotting in this cage, convinced that I was in the bowels of hell. When I was first locked down, I felt and was treated like an animal. I strolled up in here with my fingers in the air and screaming "FUCK YOU" to the world.

Welcomed by my fellow Disciples also on lockdown, a nigga like me just thought he was home.

Nigga.

That's how I used to view myself—how a lot of my black brothers view themselves. Once upon a time the white man enslaved us with that word and now we willingly do it to ourselves.

Damn shame.

Sitting up on the edge of my cot in the hell Georgia calls Jessup Federal Correctional Institution a good thirty minutes before the morning wake-up call, I can't believe this day has finally come. 'Course I haven't served nowhere near the amount of time I should. I've put to sleep a few brothas the state hasn't prosecuted me for, twelve to be exact, but I'm not the confessing type—despite my finding the road to Allah.

What can I say? Once an animal gets locked down, he only has two choices: prepare for hell or crawl in the opposite direction. I've crawled and now I'm ready to stand. I won't lie and say I'm not worried about the temptation of the street, the lure of the hustle when I leave this place. In fact, that's all I worry about since I'm leaving today.

Early release for good behavior. Now tell me that's not a sign. I'm being given another chance and this time I'm going to walk the straight and narrow and be true to my girl, Zoey.

I glance up to her picture on the wall, and I can feel a smile case around my thick lips. Zoey and I go way back. I was her first and only. We hooked up in the eighth grade when she used to hang out at my man M-Dawg's crib. I peeped her out because she curved in all the right places and knew all the words to World Famous Supreme's "Hey DJ." She tried to hold out, keep her legs closed. But after three weeks I hit a home run and rocked her world.

After that, there wasn't a damn thing she wouldn't do for me. Make a few dropoffs, get rid of a hot piece, or lie her ass off about where her man was at the time of his latest crime. I loved her for that shit.

I just didn't know it.

I might have been Zoey's one and only, but at the time she was just one of many—too many. I used women like I used drugs. They were just a temporary fix to a deeply rooted problem. Problems I denied having.

Her love scared the shit out of me. A part of me kept hoping she'd wake up and see I wasn't worth the pain. So I cheated, lied, used, and abused.

And still she remained by my side—tears and all.

So twelve murders, thirty-two robberies, countless aggravated assaults, and moving some heavy weight in and out of Bentley Manor later, here I am.

Six foot four, 235 pounds of raw muscles, I don't need a gun to put nobody's ass to sleep. But that was the old me. Folks around here now just call me Big Preacher Man. Mainly because that's all I do nowadays.

Some laugh me off, some fake the funk, trying to psych out the parole board, and others, like me, are just downright desperate for answers.

The prison guard on our block, Charlie, is almost always snarling, and now his sneer deepens. "Boys and I got a pool going on you," he says. Despite my not showing the least bit of interest, he continues. "See, I think you'll be back in here in five months. Pete says a year and Big Earl has actually bought into your Holy Rolling bullshit."

Instead of letting him bait me, I find my smile again. "Sorry, Charlie, but you're going to lose this one." I pick up my copy of the Holy Qur'an and hold it up for him. "I'm a changed man."

"Four months," he amends, laughs, and walks off to bang on the next line of bars.

As the morning rolls on, I'm surprised Charlie's words stay with me as well as his awful cackle. Around noon while I'm being processed for release, I catch sight of him again and he holds up four fingers and jiggles his eyebrows.

I shake my head. He has me all wrong.

An hour later, I'm finally handed my walking papers as well as the name and address of my new parole officer. Call me crazy, but when I walk out of there I swear the air smells fresher, tastes cleaner.

However, the best part is seeing my baby, Zoey, climb out of a silver Toyota. She's a thicker woman now. Her curves wider, her thighs and breasts larger, but her smile with the two raisin-sized dimples is still the same. While she runs toward me in a pair of tight jeans and a cloud-white, long T, I swear she's the most beautiful woman in the world.

"Demarcus!" she shouts, leaping in the air, her legs wrapping around my waist. I catch her with no problem, her warm body a welcome weight in my arms. "Oh God, baby, I can't believe this day has finally arrived." She showers kisses all over my face. The few that land on my lips are like candy that melts in your mouth. "I love you. I love you. I love you."

"I love you, too," I say and mean it. The fact that she's even here is amazing since my attempt to kill her is what landed me in the joint in the first place.

The Dealer

"Mornin', Daddy."

Lying in the middle of my silk-covered king-sized bed, I look over to the left at Suga smiling up at me and then over to my right at her sister Spyce giving me an identical smile. Twins.

I smile like the cocky motherfucker I am 'cause a nigga ain't really lived until he had two big-titty freak bitches willing to double-team his dick. Fuck Charlie, I got the real deal Angels right here waiting to fuck and suck me right.

I know I should of got them the hell out of my apartment as soon as I sprayed my nut into both of their mouths, but after that fuckin' these chicks put on me I couldn't do shit but sleep. I open one eye and look over at the Ralph Lauren digital clock on the dresser as I reach down their smooth brown bodies to palm two of the softest breasts I ever fucked with. 10:00 a.m. Shit.

They both moan as I use my fingertips to tease their

nipples until they are hard. I know I had to get some of their pussy before I roll out for the day. Fuck it.

"Suck my dick." I don't direct that shit to one or the other. It really doesn't matter, as long as I feel my tip wet soon.

They *both* shift from my arms to get on their knees on the bed and lick from the base to the thick tip. They alternate one to the other, wrapping their thick lips around my dick to suck deeply.

One and then the other. Back and forth. Each suck deeper and deeper till these bitches were deep throating me and I could feel their tonsils on my shit. Damn!

"That dick good, ain't it?" I ask them thickly, my eyes half-closed as I look at them do their work.

"Uhm-humm," they moan in unison.

I cross my feet, put my hands behind my head, and just kick back, enjoying my life as these bitches handle a dick the way it should forever and always be handled. Damn!

My doorbell sounds off just as I bite my lips to keep from hollering out as my dick pumps like a fucking gun, filling their mouths with my cum. My heart is beating and sweat is covering my body as tongues and lips suck and lick up every bit of my nut.

The doorbell sounds again as I lie stretched out in the bed, trying to breathe so that my motherfucking ass didn't stroke out or some shit. As good as they took care of that dick, it was time for business. I knew it was Usher tearing up my motherfucking doorbell.

With one last slap to their identical plush ass cheeks, I say, "Ladies, this is good. Shit, damn good, but I got work to do."

"We feel you."

"Go make that money, honey."

I slip on one of my thick-ass Hilfiger terrycloth robes and stick my feet into matching plaid slippers. "Stay here," I tell them before leaving my bedroom and closing the door behind me.

I open the front door. My best friend and right-hand man, Usher, strolls in wearing an oversized thick-ass T-shirt. I know he hot as a motherfucker in this summer heat, but fuck it, we do what we do.

As he pulls the shirt over his bald head, I open the fridge and pull out a bottle of apple juice to open and take a deep swig from. By the time I finish my drink, he has unstrapped two money belts from around his waist and dropped them onto the smoky glass table.

One hundred thousand dollars in large bills.

I reach across the table and without a word spoken, my nigga give me some dap and one of his fucked-up, crooked-teeth grins. Fuck it, what this motherfucker lacks in looks he made up for in loyalty.

I shrug and pick up the belts to hold in one hand. I love money. Always have. Always will. Even this chump change got a nigga like me happy as a motherfucker. And the hustle—my hustle—make sure the pockets stay fat.

Hustling is all I know how to do. Shit, I ain't the only one. Whether you in corporate America, busting your ass on a blue-collar nine-to-five, or going for yours in the hood, *everybody* gots a hustle. Mine is dope. Right, wrong, or indifferent . . . it is what it is and I make it do what it do. I don't gangbang. I never killed a motherfucker. I hardly ever been in a fight. I ain't angry and dangerous and that "stereotypical shit." I sling dope. Period.

And this dope game has been good to me.

Good money. Good friends. Good Life.

The Hood Life. Fuck it.

Anything I want is at the tip of my fingers, a phone call away, a shout of my voice, or the snap of my fingers. And I live my life to the fullest. The flyest gear. The dopest bitches. The baddest rides.

"Yo, Ush, I'm going back to bed. I'll get up with you later." I even throw in a stretch.

Usher just shakes his head. "Man, don't even try that bullshit with me."

I laugh 'cause he right. Feeling cocky as a motherfucker, I tie my robe a little tighter and strut my ass to my bedroom to open it wide. Suga and Spyce are dressed and sitting on the edge of the bed, waitin' to be told what to do.

I look over my shoulder as Usher walks up to me and slaps me on the back. "You a bad motherfucker."

I ain't said nothing else because there isn't shit else to be said. Not even good-bye. Usher know what the fuck is up.

Before the front door even closes behind him, I drop my robe. They here now and the coast is clear for a second. Might as well enjoy it. Fuck it.

Suga drops right to her knees and makes my dick hard as hell in her mouth as Spyce spreads my ass and licks a trail around the hole.

Stretching my arms wide, I let my head drop back and enjoy myself. Damn, life is good as hell.

Bentley Manor breeds sex, scandal, and violence. Follow four more young women who will pay any price to escape the projects.

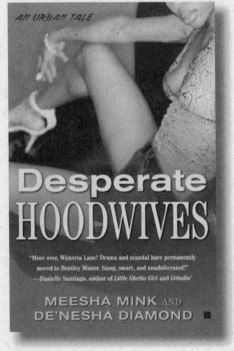

And coming in 2009, follow a pimp, a playa, a drug dealer, and a murderer in *The Hood Life*.